THE BOLO WARRIOR

BAKUNAWA RISING 2

AA LEE

Copyright © 2021 by AA Lee

All rights reserved.

No part of this book may be reproduced in any form or by any electronic or mechanical means, including information storage and retrieval systems, without written permission from the author, except for the use of brief quotations in a book review.

CONTENTS

PART I

1. The Chanter — 3
2. The Bolo Warrior — 15
3. The Chanter — 25
4. The Bolo Warrior — 39
5. The Chanter — 47
6. The Bolo Warrior — 63

PART II

7. The Chanter — 75
8. The Bolo Warrior — 83
9. The Chanter — 95
10. The Bolo Warrior — 107

PART III

11. The Chanter — 127
12. Una — 139
13. The Chanter — 149
14. Una — 163
15. The Chanter — 177
16. Una — 185
17. The Chanter — 201
18. Una — 215
19. The Chanter — 231
20. The Bolo Warrior — 243

PART I

1
THE CHANTER

There were times when Lin-ay wished she was still the secluded binukot, wished she was still sheltered from the harsh truths of the world, and wished she only chanted legends of great warriors to her people and to the future generation of binukot chanters. Today was one of those days.

Lin-ay feared that Head Warrior Kidlat would banish them as soon as they arrived at the barangay. Makanas had defied his father and followed Lin-ay to make sure she was safe on her mission to save her brother. Perhaps Kidlat would forgive them because they had recovered the stolen blades that could kill Bakunawa, the giant moon-eating serpent. Still, she dreaded facing the head warrior. She had struck him with a magical sword before she left the barangay.

"We really have to get back to the barangay. I've been away for far too long, and we don't have much time left before the full moon." Ready to fly, Makanas lifted his chin as he took Lin-ay's hand.

"We still have two weeks left, Makanas," Bugna said, eyeing the bakunawa blade on Makanas's waist. The shaman's serene face belied the dread Lin-ay knew they all felt.

Lin-ay had refused to touch the weapon. The last time she held it, the moon goddess had taken over her body. Her mind raced. The quiet forest didn't help her reach a decision. Even the cicadas were quiet, as though they knew that Bugna was having a serious conversation. If she stayed here in Sulod, Bugna could help her control her emotions and power when she held the bakunawa blade, but her brother was in the barangay.

Bugna continued, "If you can awaken the bakunawa blade before then…"

Makanas let out a forced smile. "It will kill. That's all I need."

"Tell Kidlat I'll do my best to piece them together"—on the grass lay the two fragments of the blade that Datu Habagat had wielded and Lin-ay had smashed into pieces when Bulan took over her body—"but I could no longer do a unification with the other four. There's no time to gather the required anting-antings in two weeks. Ah! I have an idea." Bugna bent down and picked up one of the pieces by its the point. She rose in the air and held it up to Lin-ay. "Perhaps this'll help you."

Lin-ay hesitated. Although small, that was still a part of the bakunawa blade. Bugna held her hand steady. Lin-ay decided to accept it, resolving to throw it the moment Bulan tried to enter her mind. She ripped a strip from her already-torn skirt, wrapped the piece of metal with it, and secured it in a pocket.

Bugna's smile was radiant. Even her pristine dress seemed to glow. "If we survive Bakunawa's rising, I'd love to attend your wedding."

Lin-ay yanked her hand away from Makanas as if she was touching fire. Heat rose to her cheeks as her feet touched the ground again. "We're not—"

"Okay…" Bugna grinned. "Hurry now, will you? Kidlat must be pacing back and forth now like there's fire in his ass."

Lin-ay scratched her head. Unlike Makanas, she had no anting-anting to let her fly. Eyes glued to the ground, she held a hand up toward Makanas.

"Are you sure you know where you're going?" Bugna laughed. "Focus! You're running around like headless chickens. Didn't I tell you you can't get out of here by air?"

Lin-ay withdrew her hand. She turned west, but dreaded the thought of traveling out of the enchanted Sulod forest alone with Makanas. White sampaguita flowers surrounded Bugna's house and soft grass carpeted her wide yard, but weeks before, they were snared by illusions set by Bugna when they entered the forest. The shaman's spell was designed to prevent intruders from finding her or her house.

"Just get them out of here!" Putot shouted from the

back of Mimi, her gigantic white feline companion, as he strolled out of Bugna's house. "I'll keep watch."

Bugna lifted a hand. In a blink, Lin-Ay, Makanas, and she were out of Sulod. Bugna gently lowered a hand and Makanas and Lin-ay landed on the river bank. "May the good spirits help us so we'll see each other again in two weeks." With that, Bugna disappeared.

Makanas held Lin-ay's hand and flew in silence. Not knowing how to talk to him, Lin-ay preferred it that way. Thankfully, the awkwardness faded as they reached the barangay, which felt empty save for the children looking down the rice terraces from the edges of the plateau.

"What about the children?" Lin-ay asked. The Bolo Warrior Barangay's children trained to fight from the age of eight, but she hoped they would be spared of the responsibility to fight in the upcoming war.

"They have to evacuate. Maybe this week. There's a place designated for them and the old men and women."

"Lin-ay!" Ten-year-old Kayay ran toward her, her cheeks flushed. "Head Warrior Kidlat told us to get you down when you arrive."

"Down where?"

"Down there." Kayay pointed at her feet. "I can get you there."

"Don't worry," Makanas said. "I'll take her there."

Kayay bowed to Makanas. "But… the boy."

"Where is he?" Lin-ay asked. When Kayay pointed

toward the communal kitchen, Lin-ay dashed off, barely hearing Makanas saying he was heading to the meeting hall. She heard her brother's sobs before she saw him. "Adlaw?"

The boy's red eyes met hers. "Lin-ay." The boy wrapped his arms around Lin-ay's waist, his tears soaking through her shirt. "I want to go home."

Her brother had lost weight, and his smiling eyes were hollow with grief. He had seen too much suffering and death at such a young age. Lin-ay caressed his oily hair and wondered if the boy had even learned to take a bath on his own. The boy had lived in the city for more than a moon when the foreigners called *pangayaws* had attacked Lin-ay's barangay and killed her parents. Fortunately, a *pari* took him before he could be sold as a slave.

"So do I." But no home existed for them anymore. "When I rescue Mother, we will have our own house. We'll find Suga and the rest of your attendants."

"And my friends too?" Adlaw's eyes lit with excitement.

"I will try, but for now, a bigger enemy is coming. Bigger than the evil Miguel. We must defeat it first, or it will kill all the people in this barangay." *Dear spirits, help me keep my promise.*

"I don't like the people here. They all look scary."

"No, we're not," said Kayay, who'd entered the communal kitchen unnoticed. "Stop being a crybaby. You're eight."

Adlaw cast his eyes downward. "I'm not a crybaby."

"Yes, you are. You're crying like a baby," Kayay said, drawing closer.

"I'm not!" Adlaw balled his fists, tears brimming in his eyes.

"Enough!" Lin-ay's words came sharper than intended, making the two children freeze. "I'm sorry. Kayay, where's Inday?"

"In the meeting hall," Kayay said as she tucked a lock of hair behind her ear. The child still looked elegant despite her rigorous early-morning training as the future Bolo Warrior Barangay's warrior.

Lin-ay suddenly felt self-conscious. Her feet were caked with dirt, and her skirt was torn.

"She'd been waiting for you like a hen, walking to and fro since this morning." Kayay led them as though she was the oldest in the group. "She was muttering like a madwoman too. Something about a *binukot* being with a man is insane. That's what I heard."

Inday sighed with relief as Lin-ay entered the meeting hall. "Dear spirits, binukot, what took you so long?" Her former head attendant still acted like Lin-ay was a helpless, secluded woman. "I thought… May Master Bangkaw forgive me, but I can't help but think about the dangers in Sulod."

Lin-ay waved a hand to dismiss Inday's concern. "Bugna is on our side. We shouldn't be afraid of her."

"Oh, dear spirits. You met the immortal shaman?" When Adlaw sniffed and wiped the last drop of tears from his cheeks, Inday seemed to notice the boy and used the hem of her blouse to wipe the boy's nose. "Ah.

This plateau is awfully cold in the morning. You better wait until sunrise before you go out, or your nose will turn into a river."

"Here," Kayay held out a handkerchief embroidered with white sampaguita flowers. "He should wipe his own nose."

Adlaw's cheeks flushed, but he snatched the handkerchief out of Kayay's hand.

"Master Adlaw, go and eat sugarcane with Libon." When the boy shook his head, Inday crouched low and put a gold coin in his palm. "Tell him to cut as many as he can and that Lin-ay has returned."

Adlaw bobbed his head and ran toward the door, Kayay hot on his heels.

Lin-ay shook her head, dumbfounded. "That boy didn't care about gold."

Inday shrugged. "He obviously cares now, after all his jewelry was taken away." When Lin-ay sighed, Inday sighed in return. "Don't worry, he'll get along with other kids here just fine. Kayay seem to do a good job at keeping him occupied."

"This way." Makanas was putting stones in the wall.

Lin-ay hadn't noticed the man when she entered. As she drew closer, she noticed holes in the wall. Each stone had a distinct shape that matched a hole. Makanas placed the stones without looking. He must have done that countless times. When he finally finished filling the holes, Lin-ay realized they formed a pattern of the bakunawa blade. Lin-ay gasped as the floor moved before them and a square opened, revealing spiral stairs made of stones passing through perhaps more than a hundred floors. On either side, orbs of white light made it look like the sun was reaching underground.

Makanas led them downward, his footsteps echoing. He completed another puzzle that looked like the one above by putting stones into the wall, and the portal above them slammed shut.

Lin-ay followed Makanas down the stairs. Just thinking about the mountain's height was enough to make her head spin. She held onto the handrail tight.

"Better than torches cause they don't run out." Makanas said as he caught Lin-ay staring at the white orbs.

Lin-ay nodded in agreement. "Just a moment." She released a long breath as she leaned against the wall of the top floor. Her knees had started to shake. They continued heading downward after a short break. Very soon, she saw the barangay people coming out of the stone rooms. Most of them were carrying sacks on their shoulders. The lower they got, the busier it became. "Weapons?" Lin-ay asked.

"No. Food. This mountain is connected to another mountain through an underground pass. We don't want our enemies to see where the women and children will hide."

"It's a miracle this mountain doesn't collapse, with all the holes in here." Despite the fact that everything she saw was made of rock, the thought of the mountain collapsing with all the people inside terrified her.

"Bugna helped build this mountain," Makanas said.

"Build?"

"In here!" Una opened one of the biggest doors Lin-ay had seen yet. "Welcome back, anting-anting hunter!" She slapped Lin-ay's shoulder so hard Lin-ay staggered back.

Lin-ay couldn't help but smile at the sight of the warrior and Makanas's closest friend. She entered the room, glad to rest her shaky knees. Head Warrior Kidlat's scarred face greeted her. Behind him was Head Guard Uwak, smiling like a father welcoming his son back after a war. In contrast, the head warrior, and Makanas's father, was hard to read. Lin-ay bowed deep, guilt gnawing at her for having attacked Kidlat. She braced for a punishment and kept her head low.

"Great work," Kidlat said.

Lin-ay straightened. She waited for the head warrior to pronounce their punishment, but he only stared at the bakunawa on Makanas's waist.

"We have five now. Datu Habagat and Dungog don't stand a chance against us," Head Guard Uwak said, admiring the Bakunawa-head-shaped hilt of Makanas's blade.

"Seven. It might take some time for Bugna to fix the other two." Makanas bowed low to his father then narrated everything that had happened. He sounded like he was reciting something from a book he'd read.

"Even better!" Kidlat smacked Makanas's shoulder, the sound making Lin-ay flinch. "In that case, you might want to lend the blade to Lin-ay."

"No," Lin-ay croaked. "I'm not ready."

"No one is, but Bakunawa will rise either way." Head Warrior Kidlat stretched out a hand and received the blade from Makanas. "I need your help. You're the only one who can detect an anting-anting."

"I don't need the blade anymore," Lin-Ay said.

Head Warrior Kidlat raised an eyebrow.

"I... I can sense them now without it."

Lin-ay hadn't thought about it but was just realizing that fact. Before, she had needed the blade to see anting-antings, but as she looked around, inspecting each of the warrior's anting-antings in the room, her sense of them became even more acute. Before, she could only sense them based on the intensity of their glow, but presently, they seemed to pulse as if alive. She could even sense them without looking. After having used the bakunawa blade the day before, her body seemed to have changed. Too much power was in one place, like noises competing with each other. Lin-ay tried her best to concentrate on the most powerful one and to ignore the rest. Then she remembered the broken bakunawa blade point in her pocket. "Oh!"

"Well and good," Kidlat said. "But Makanas didn't awaken the blade. It would be more powerful in your hands."

Lin-ay shook her head again. "I can't right now."

"Fine." The head warrior's voice was sharper than any blade. "But I need you here on the day of Bakunawa's rising. I will be in the east sea to battle with the serpent. You will be the eyes and ears of the warriors. If they know who has the most powerful anting-anting, they can target them first."

"I can do that," Lin-ay said.

Her eyes wandered around the room full of weapons, whose long barrels faced the walls, tips extending outward. The walls had tiny holes just large enough to see through, save for the ones where barrels met stone. She'd studied the weaponry in books but hadn't expected to see it in person. She was more surprised at Head Warrior Kidlat's acceptance of the foreign weapons.

"This room is Head Guard Uwak's station. It's connected by holes meant to carry sounds to other rooms, so when you tell them where an incoming enemy is, you don't need to run around."

Head Guard Uwak dipped his head in acknowledgement at the mention of his name.

"I can see and tell whether an anting-anting is powerful or not, but I've never been in a war. I'm not sure I can do it. What if I fail?" *Or if Bulan takes over my body?* Lin-ay still couldn't think of the goddess as herself, and referring to her as a separate entity was easier.

"Then the warriors will fight as we've trained for years, trusting expertise, eyes, and ears. But your talent will play a crucial role, so I hope we can set aside our differences and focus on this." The Head Warrior's eyes met hers, unwavering. "And if you can call Bulan, even better."

Something occurred to Lin-ay. The head warrior had

expressed his hatred of Bulan before and said the goddess had abandoned humans. But now, his nonchalant attitude about her calling the goddess bothered her.

"You have the blade now, but you're still helping me," she said. "With all the trouble I've caused this barangay, I don't believe you're just trying to please my father in the afterlife. Why? Why are you helping me? And don't try to fool me. I will find out eventually, just as I found out you weren't planning to rescue my brother and mother."

She expected the head warrior to apologize, but he remained stoic. She wondered if the emotions he'd shown before were merely masks to hide his real face.

"Because Bugna told me the only chance of defeating Bakunawa is to keep you by my side."

2

THE BOLO WARRIOR

Makanas shifted his gaze from Kidlat to Lin-ay. He thought Kidlat was only after Lin-ay's bakunawa blade. Lin-ay had been sheltered all her life and had just started training to fight with the children. He scratched his head and cursed Bugna for hiding the fact from him. *It wouldn't have made a difference. I'm only following father's orders.* Maybe Bugna didn't trust him. Perhaps, the shaman thought Makanas would hide Lin-ay from his father.

"How…? It doesn't make sense." Lin-ay crossed her arms across her chest.

"I tried, believe me," Kidlat said. "But Bugna doesn't control what she can see. She can't tell how you will help, only that you need to be here."

Lin-ay tilted her head. "I don't know. I'm afraid I will only get in the way."

"Now that you're back, how about a test?" Kidlat asked.

"A test?" Lin-ay squeaked.

"Of your ability. Let's have some warriors flying far enough for you not to see their faces. Are you sure you don't need the blade?"

Makanas's hand tightened around the hilt of the bakunawa but pretended to be undoing the tie around his waist. Showing his interest in the blade might prompt his father to take it away. From a young age, he'd learned how to hide his emotions.

Lin-ay shook her head vigorously. Makanas wanted to sigh in relief but stopped himself. He wanted a chance to practice with the blade. Although guilt gnawed at him for keeping the blade for himself, he believed Lin-ay didn't need the sword. For her, a goddess was but a prayer away.

"Then let's start." Kidlat held up a black cloth.

As Lin-ay tied the cloth around her head, Makanas and other warriors flew up and out from the underground. He circled high around the mountain until a round-headed arrow hit his leg. He grunted and spiraled down together with the anting-anting-powered arrow. He managed to right himself before hitting the ground. No way could Lin-ay have seen his face from that far away. Wondering if the head guard would shoot him again, he rose through the air. *Down*, he whistled in their bird language.

"Damn! That hurt!" Una shouted. The woman raised a hand in surrender. "Does that mean I'm just a bit less powerful than you?" she asked as Baskog also

The Bolo Warrior

fell like a bird. "Looks like they're starting with the most powerful."

"Maybe," Makanas shrugged as he landed on the plateau.

"Can't believe I'm stronger than Baskog."

They descended into the underground and found Lin-ay pointing upward. She had no sense of direction, so Head Guard Uwak was relying on her hand.

"There," she said. "The headscarf is the most powerful."

Makanas peeked through a hole and saw another warrior fall from the sky. "Incredible."

"They're all down." Lin-ay peeled the cloth away.

"That was spectacular, Lin-ay." Kidlat clapped his hands together once. The head warrior rarely clapped, and when he did, the compliment was genuine.

"Thank you." Lin-ay bowed.

"But our warriors will be flying with them too. If only we have time to hunt for an anting-anting that could aid your vision."

Makanas scratched his head. He hadn't thought of that before. His father, as always, was a master planner.

"Perhaps she could get acquainted with our warriors' anting-antings," Makanas said. "We have time."

"Exactly." Kidlat gestured with a hand. "With your acute senses, it'll probably take less than a week for you to tell them apart. You only need to remember those who can fly."

"There's more than a hundred of them," Lin-ay said,

shaking her head a little. The girl might not even know all their names.

"How about…" Makanas paused as all heads turned toward him. He was used to all the warriors listening to his father, but not to him. He swallowed, praying his voice didn't sound too high. When his father gave a slight nod, he continued, "Giving all of them the same anting-antings. Perhaps weak ones that would help you distinguish them from the enemies."

"A good plan." Kidlat nodded, obviously giving the suggestion a careful thought. "But not foolproof. While we're at it, you should work on sensing their main anting-antings." When Lin-ay bowed and turned to go, Kidlat turned to Makanas. "Anything you want to tell me about Datu Habagat?"

Makanas was rather surprised at the way his father was talking to him, having expected a private punishment. "He has a thousand-year-old shaman who could act as a medium. It allowed Datu Habagat to use his magic on the person despite the distance."

Kidlat didn't speak.

"But Putot has been freed."

Kidlat's eyes widened. "Good. But he has more."

Makanas tilted his head. "You knew about this?" *Yet you sent me on my first mission to the datu anyway?*

"I knew he wouldn't kill you."

Makanas saw red. *Ruthless. You don't know how painful it was.* His hand gripped the bakunawa blade.

"I'll give you the chance to cut off his head," Kidlat said, turning toward the wall and reassessing the weapons, his eyes searching. "No. You must kill him. He killed your mother. It's only right. And since you'll be the future head warrior of this barangay, his head will serve as a warning to those who would question your authority."

"Thank you," Makanas said, the heat of his anger dissipating. He would gladly cut the evil datu limb from limb and make sure he would never rise again. "And he has something that suppresses anting-antings' power."

Kidlat whirled around. "How strong?"

"Everything stopped working. I couldn't feel a thing, and even Lin-ay failed to call Bulan."

"He's much stronger now but couldn't be stronger than the blades."

"You knew?"

Makanas stepped back as realization dawned on him that his father, despite not having left the forests for years, had a wider knowledge than he, who'd spent most of his teenage life on missions. Kidlat might even have his own tracker or the anting-anting suppressor. With his power to shut off one anting-anting like it was simply breathing, Makanas wouldn't be surprised if Kidlat had been hiding the suppressor all along. But the tracker would be hard to hide. He needed a shaman.

"Head Warrior"—Head Guard Uwak dipped his head—"if this datu could suppress anting-antings, our entire defense could fail."

"Two concealers won't work when activated at the same place." Kidlat stared at Makanas's balled fists and sighed as though Makanas was a child acting up. "He'll come after me first. What's with that face, warrior?" he roared. When Makanas dipped his head and straightened, Kidlat nodded and was the emotionless head warrior again. "Follow me."

Makanas floated behind his father, following the spiral stairs downward and stopping midway. Makanas had helped the warriors strategize weapons placement in hundreds of rooms, but the one Kidlat approached was a room Makanas hadn't been inside since he was eight. Makanas wondered why they were headed to the prison cell. They'd had no prisoners since having settled on the plateau, and Makanas suspected Kidlat simply killed those banished criminals they'd caught. In their ten years of living in the Bolo Warrior Barangay, two spies had been cast out, and Makanas never heard of them again. A narrow passageway zigzagged like a puzzle from the first door. A few turns later, they faced a smaller and narrower door with no windows or even a tiny hole let light in. When Kidlat locked them both inside, he understood why.

"All corners of this room have been sealed by anting-anting concealers. Now that you know what kind of power Datu Habagat has, I think it is time you see this." Kidlat stepped out and grabbed one of the bright orbs.

Even with the light, Makanas couldn't distinguish the room from any others, except for its emptiness. "But why didn't we hunt any of this type of anting-antings?"

"Because we can't." Kidlat drew closer to one corner

of the room. "The cave to the underworld is guarded by beasts and Bakunawa where he is stronger. What little dark magic remains in the world of the living was passed on when the gate was open."

"You mean this is an evil magic."

"Magic depends on the user. The source is no matter."

"But why are you telling me this?"

"Because Datu Habagat has a concealer in his body. It's not something you can simply take from him. It has completely merged with his body. That's why all those who are after his life failed. If I die, I need you to carve out the concealer in me and fight him."

"Carve?" Makanas was repulsed by the thought. He didn't shy away from violence, but violating a dead man's body was beyond him.

"You must do it," Kidlat said, anger rising at Makanas's weakness again.

"You can kill—"

Kidlat raised a hand and tilted his head, focused on a bird call from the guards. "Amihan?"

Makanas flew up the tunnel before his father could say anything. He heard Kidlat whistle, ordering the guards to bring Amihan up to the Bolo Warrior Barangay. He glided above the children racing toward the edge of the plateau. The guards carrying Amihan were heading toward the meeting hall. "No! Put her down there." He pointed at a foot-tall ceremonial table by the edge of the plateau. He hadn't closed the entrance to the underground. Amihan was a stranger, and even though she's Lin-ay's mother, he didn't know her well.

Makanas barely recognized Amihan. Ragged clothes covered her frail, bruised body. He flew close, hoping his healing anting-anting could keep her alive.

"Where is she?" Iyay ran like she was twenty years younger, a few vials dropping out of her open bag. "Hold her up. Make her sit." She motioned at Makanas. "And somebody get Lin-ay for me, quick!"

Makanas met Una's eyes and gave her the order without a word. He pulled Amihan into a sitting position and leaned her against his body. "Wait."

He gently pushed up Amihan's sleeve. Two puncture marks stared back at him, a clear message that the barangay needed to know.

"The woman cannot wait." Iyay held a spoon closer to Amihan's mouth, her bony hands steady, and her eyes clear with determination to save Amihan. "It looks like she hasn't eaten for days."

"She probably wanted to die in the forest." Makanas smoothed Amihan's sleeve back down.

"Nobody's dying on my watch. Hold her mouth open."

Makanas tilted the woman's head back to force her to swallow. Una flew back, holding Lin-ay's hand.

Lin-ay scrambled toward Amihan. "Mother! Thanks the spirits you escaped."

Makanas wanted to say she hadn't escaped but swallowed his words, letting the girl believe for a moment that her mother was free.

Amihan's eyelids cracked open slowly. "I shouldn't."

"What?" Lin-ay leaned in closer.

"Carry me out of here before he returns," Amihan pleaded as she tried to catch her breath.

Makanas swooped in to carry her, but Lin-ay grabbed his hand. "What are you doing?"

"You heard her." Makanas gently peeled Lin-ay's hands away. "Dungog or Datu Habagat could be watching us right now."

With trembling hands, Amihan rolled up her sleeves, baring the two bite marks for the barangay people who had gathered around to see. Confused eyes stared at her, but Makanas knew Lin-ay understood what those bite marks meant.

"B-but she's sick. You can't simply banish her. She'll die." Her eyes swirled with emotions—perhaps joy at rejoining with her mother, but fear too, and sadness.

Makanas needed to decide—quickly. He wondered what was taking his father so long to show up. Makanas had limited knowledge about trackers, and he couldn't bring Amihan to the underground prison. *Would wooden bars work?* He certainly didn't feel that Datu Habagat could use his magic through him when Makanas had a tracker in him, but he'd spoken through him before and even shut his mouth when he tried to warn others about his condition. And pain was more than enough motivation to make Makanas do things he didn't like. Amihan choosing pain and death spoke to how strong the woman was.

"Bring us together." Lin-ay stared at him with pleading eyes before he could come up with a solution. "With my anting-anting, she won't feel pain, at least."

Lin-ay couldn't have been more wrong. Even with the girl holding her mother's hand, Amihan squeezed her eyes shut and writhed in pain. Iyay opened bottle after bottle, rubbing oils and powders availing nothing. Lin-ay took the ylang-ylang from her pocket and pressed it against Amihan's forehead. The tracker was different from Putot's. Even if they called Putot, who knew about tracker magic, the warriors could take weeks to enter Sulod, and bringing Amihan to Sulod would mean opening the forest to either Dungog or Datu Habagat.

"Inay!" Adlaw cried as he entered the meeting hall.

Kayay pulled him back upon seeing Amihan's situation. The two kids struggled, but Adlaw was no match for Kayay's strength.

"Where's the Head Warrior?" Makanas asked.

Una shook her head. "He didn't want Datu Habagat to sense his anting-anting."

Makanas pressed his temples in frustration. His father would let Amihan die, but surely, Datu Habagat didn't want her to perish that early. He'd sent her on purpose. Healing anting-antings didn't work. His last resort was to end her life quickly to stop her suffering, but he lacked the courage to reveal that resolution to Lin-ay.

3

THE CHANTER

Tears streamed down Lin-ay's face as Amihan's cries of agony went on for hours. Her mother, the strongest authority she'd known since she was young, was begging for the pain to stop. She promised to kill Datu Habagat and make him pay for putting a tracker on her.

"What do you want?" Lin-ay asked the question not of her mother, but of Datu Habagat.

Amihan stopped writhing. The meeting hall went dead still except for the loud drumming of Lin-ay's heart.

Amihan's eyes opened, calm despite the tears. In a steady voice, she said, "Pay me a visit, Binukot." The words weren't Datu Habagat's but Dungog's. "Do you like my present? You don't have to lift a finger. She's free... but of course, with a price, as with all things here on earth."

"Why do you want me?" Of course, she knew.

"I found the perfect husband for you, Binukot. Datu Habagat." Dungog laughed that wheezy laugh that fooled people into believing he was nothing but an old, frail elder.

Lin-ay knew she shouldn't negotiate with the old man, who was as sly as a fox, but she didn't have a choice. That was the only way to stop Amihan's pain. She knew, too, that the marriage was just a diversion. Habagat might not even want her.

"I will go," she said.

"Good thinking, my dear." Amihan sat up straight. "And hurry. Let's say… you have to be here in less than a week. Enough time for Kidlat to decide. If I don't see you here in a week, Amihan will join her husband in the afterlife. You must come untainted."

Lin-ay flushed with embarrassment. In her periphery, she saw Makanas clenching his fists. She wanted to curse Dungog, to pray to the evil spirits to take him, but right then, no one could help her but herself. "I understand. But let my mother be. Give me exactly a week."

"I'm busy, dear. I don't want to spend my time spying on you, for I know you will come." Amihan's head dipped, and without Makanas supporting her, she would have dropped to the ground.

"Mother!" Lin-ay gently shook Amihan's shoulders.

"Don't go. Dungog knows who you are. He's going to use you to get Bakunawa's power and then yours too."

"My power?" She'd thought Dungog was only after her marriage. Then she remembered Bugna's prophecy, revealed to her by Kidlat. Of course, Dungog wanted her away from the barangay to stop the prophecy. He wanted Bakunawa's power for himself. The tension in her shoulders eased as the bruises on Amihan's face disappeared. Dungog must have left her mind, allowing the healing anting-anting to work.

"Bulan's power," Amihan said. "Hasn't Bugna told you yet?"

Iyay mumbled some incomprehensible words.

Lin-ay knew the old woman was trying to distract her. "No. Tell me."

"Oh, dear spirits. Shamans and their unbelievable play with words." Amihan righted herself and sat cross-legged as color returned to her pale cheeks. She looked around the warriors around her. "You are Bulan. The reason I raised you as a binukot was because I didn't want you to merge with your spirit and because I didn't know Bakunawa would return in your lifetime. If your spirit returns, you could die, and the spirit would take over. You will become a shell."

Complete silence filled the meeting hall. Lin-ay wanted to say Amihan was just kidding, and perhaps she had found humor amidst the pain she was suffering. But Amihan didn't laugh or smile.

"I'm sorry, Lin-ay." Amihan used her name, not *binukot* or *dearie* or *child*. That meant she wanted Lin-ay to remember every word she said. "When I first met Bugna, she told me a story I would never forget. That story made me accept Bulan's offer to bear you."

Lin-ay held her breath, her eyes never leaving her

mother's face. Her heart drummed. She sensed that after this story, she would be changed forever.

"A long time ago," Amihan started, "shamans equaled the power of the gods of the lower pantheon. Shamans like Bulan walked among the gods. They envied the gods' power and started a revolution. Of course, they were no match against the gods, especially those of the higher pantheon. That was until Bulan took their side. She led other gods of the lower pantheon. They were mostly half humans who didn't want the people on earth obliterated."

Lin-ay wanted to ask why Bathala let it happen, but just the thought of questioning Bathala made her tremble. The supreme ruler of the gods could strike her just for questioning his power.

As if Amihan had read Lin-ay's mind, she said, "Bathala started noticing the revolution when the gods fought each other. He sealed the earth, and the only way for gods to enter was through the lake of life, which he controls. And then he punished Bulan."

"That is…" Lin-ay tried to think of a subtle word to use.

"Unfair," Amihan completed her sentence.

"Mother!" Lin-ay shouted as the others in the meeting hall gasped at once, making it feel like they'd inhaled all the air.

"Oh, forget it. Bugna curses Bathala all the time. We're nothing but a nuisance like dust to him. If we stir, it is a bother to him. I think Bugna is trying to get his attention when she curses, but she hasn't succeeded so far."

"So what was Bulan's punishment?" Lin-ay asked.

"She was cut in two. Her human soul was sent here on Earth, and her spirit, that is, the one that has her powers, was imprisoned in the gods' realm. The last bit of her power was sent to the moon because she is the goddess of the moon. Each time her soul was reborn, Bathala released her spirit. She will only succeed at merging again when the human body is strong both physically and mentally. If the human body and mind is weak, it'll kick the soul out, and the body will be a shell. Bulan's spirit is… violent. She was the goddess of war, after all. I didn't want you to become a shell. That's why I raised you as a binukot."

"So that's why Bakunawa is trying to swallow the moon. He was after Bulan's power."

"That is what we know, but I believe there could be more. But there's no way of telling for sure because Bulan talked to Bugna when her soul was about to leave her mortal body. She regains some of her memories when she is in the afterlife."

"Bugna again?" Lin-ay asked. "Why is Bugna entangled in all this?"

"Bulan… or should I say you… were once Bugna's daughter. Bugna borrowed your face so she wouldn't forget you as time passes by."

"But why me?" Lin-ay asked. "I'm not strong. I don't know ceremonies or call on the gods' help.

"Not you. Me. Bulan appeared in my dream the

night I killed my suitor. She... or should I say... you told me to take your father as my husband."

"I thought the suitor disappeared."

Amihan moved a hand up and down her arm, an unconscious habit when discussing uncomfortable topics. "Yes. With Bugna's help. But I spilled his blood for attempting to force himself on me."

Lin-ay squeezed her eyes shut and covered them with her hands. The revelations were too much. They felt like blinding lights keeping her from seeing what she needed to. "You must tell me about Dungog's anting-antings."

"No. I will die before he gets his hands on you. He teamed up with Habagat—those two vile demons." Amihan's voice was like a whip, sharp and quick. She was the strong and composed mentor again.

"Mother, I have a god in me. I'm Bulan, and her power is at my disposal. Don't be afraid." She still doubted that she was truly Bulan's reborn soul, but for now, she needed to accept it and show her mother so that she would have confidence in her.

"It would be best to leave the fighting to Kidlat. You are not ready in that unprepared body."

"Wait..." Lin-ay said. "Unprepared body? You mean there's a way for me to prepare so I can merge with my spirit without turning into a shell?"

"Yes." Amihan released a deep sigh. "But I never thought I'd tell you this."

"How?" Lin-ay asked, her voice rising.

Had she still been a binukot, Amihan might have scolded and perhaps punished her.

"Magic. What better way to get closer to a god than using magic? You must acquire, train, and use anting-antings to strengthen your body and soul. Bugna should've told you about this already."

"But we have no time."

"Exactly. So leave the god business to Kidlat. Don't attempt to negotiate with Dungog."

"Your mother's right," Makanas said. "For now, let's find a way to remove the tracker in her."

The truth poured over Lin-ay like a waterfall. She had been so overwhelmed about Bulan that she'd forgotten her mother almost died just moments before. "Right. We must remove it." She couldn't look Makanas in the eye and tell him the best way was to follow Dungog's order and marry another man. She glanced at her mother, afraid that Dungog was watching from behind her eyes.

"I can't feel his presence. He's not watching now." Amihan said as she stood on steady legs.

"What else did Bulan tell you?" Lin-ay asked.

"She is a half human who'd been outcast by other gods." Amihan shook her head in disappointment. "Even talking to humans was limited. If she could have, I know she had a lot to say."

Something nagged at the back of Lin-ay's head. "Mother, who injected the tracker?" She realized that if they knew who that was, rescuing the shaman and having the tracker removed would be easier.

"I didn't see. Dungog had me blindfolded, but before I lost consciousness, I saw a crocodile and a snake. I'm quite sure the crocodile was Dungog, but this..." She touched her arm. "I'm sure it was done by a snake."

"We have to see Putot." Lin-ay turned to Makanas.

Makanas nodded and turned to Amihan. "I'm sorry, but for now, I need you guarded."

"I want to see my son." Amihan said.

Lin-ay journeyed back to Sulod with Dasig to get Putot. Kidlat had expressed his surrender, saying they had no way to get the shaman who'd injected the tracker into Amihan. Putot could inject tracker magic into people and control them, so Lin-ay hoped the shaman could help them get rid of Dungog's tracker.

"Slow down, Lin-ay," Dasig said behind her. The man was faster than she but had been slowing down to stay behind her. Before they left the barangay, Dasig had assured Makanas he would protect Lin-ay with his life. Makanas trusted Dasig, and had assured his father he wouldn't abandon his duty by staying in the barangay.

"We have to get there before sunset." Lin-ay's sore legs were protesting. She slowed down and jammed a sweet potato into her mouth. They couldn't afford to stop and rest. Flying into Sulod was a sure way to get lost, so Dasig had landed just outside the tree tunnel, and they had run from there. She had seven days, and if Putot couldn't help, they would be down to six. Thankfully, Bugna's spells that created illusions to stop intruders from entering her domain had completely disappeared.

She skidded to a halt when a blinding light assaulted her eyes. She knew the path, but a gigantic tree appeared where she'd never seen it before. She covered her eyes with her hands and squinted. The sun itself appeared to have descended to the earth. The whole tree, shimmering and golden from root to leaves, pulsed with life. On one of the branches sat an eagle, protecting a nest of even brighter broken eggshells. Brown feathers adorned its head like a crown, befitting its nickname as the king of birds. Its blue-gray raptor eyes bore through her. The eagle was smaller than Agila but still taller than Lin-ay. *Anting-anting.* She needed to get those eggshells.

"What is it?" Dasig asked, hands on the hilt of his bolo blade.

Lin-ay pointed up at the eagle.

Dasig shook his head. "I don't see anything."

"The tree. Up! Look at the eagle."

Dasig closed his eyes for a moment and opened them again. "Perhaps another trick? Maybe another illusion we haven't encountered before."

"Impossible. The tree's hiding it." Lin-ay ran her fingers around the inch-long broken tip of the bakunawa blade in her pocket. She'd expected some distractions as it allowed her to sense anting-antings, but she'd never thought it would allow her to see invisible creatures. While she wasn't certain, she had a feeling she could gain two crucial powers —flight from the shells and invisibility from the tree. But the eagle might kill her if she attempted to steal the eggshells it protected. Her eyes moved from the eagle and the orange sky in the west. The day was almost over. Time—she needed more time.

"We could come back here with Kidlat. He could help you." Dasig grasped Lin-ay's hand and pulled her back.

Had she still been a binukot, she would have slapped his hand away. Lin-ay banished the thought of her former status. She was a Bolo Barangay Warrior trainee, and she must not recoil from people's touch.

Kidlat wouldn't bother with anting-anting hunting —not until he slayed Bakunawa, at least. He had all the power he needed. But Lin-ay needed power, something that could help her body get used to Bulan's power, as her mother had said. Invisibility might not be able to fool Dungog and Datu Habagat, but she could at least slip past his guards. And the flight the eagle shells would give her would help her travel without dragging a warrior along.

The eagle was unusually still for a magical bird protecting its nest. It should've attacked them already, as was the tendency of creatures that didn't want humans to take whatever magic was left in their previous bodies. Lin-ay marched forward, pulling

Dasig along. The magical eagle spread its wings, perhaps certain that Lin-ay could indeed see it.

Lin-ay climbed the gnarled roots, hugging the tree trunk like a person bracing against a cold wind.

"I-it's not an illusion." Dasig crouched and touched the root in front of him. He might have seen the determination in Lin-ay's eyes, for he straightened his slouched, lean body. "Tell me what you see." After Lin-ay detailed the invisible bird and tree, Dasig cut off a portion of his loincloth and covered his eyes. "You'll be eyes. Wait. Did it just flap its wings?" When Lin-ay confirmed, he said, "At least I can use my ears," and smiled.

As Dasig climbed, roots snaked up his legs. Lin-ay ducked and stepped back as Dasig hacked at the roots. They slowly climbed up, swallowing his body. What he couldn't see was that the faster he cut, the faster the roots grew back. Lin-ay grabbed the hilt of her bolo blade to help Dasig but then let it fall back into its sheath. She didn't sense evil in the tree. In fact, the glow prompted her to only think of doing good to others.

So why is it swallowing us? "Stop!" Lin-ay shouted.

She had to repeat herself several times before Dasig listened. The moment he stopped hacking at the tree, the roots stopped moving.

"Sheathe your sword."

Dasig froze in stunned disbelief.

"Slowly sheathe your sword."

"I must have accidentally stabbed it," Dasig said, breathing deeply as the roots retreated.

Lin-ay didn't share his relief. She had no way to get a part of the tree without triggering a reaction. Invisibility was powerful, but she could do without it for the time being. She had to focus on the flying magic.

Dasig climbed the tree, and Lin-ay followed every crevice he'd used to support his weight. Her muscles trembled with the effort. The eagle flapped its wings, and Lin-ay's hold broke. Dasig held her up, his other hand holding onto the first branch. The whole forest shook at the eagle's piercing cry. It flapped its wings again, and Dasig and Lin-ay thudded against the ground like rocks. Then the eagle descended like a mountain, its sharp talons ready to pierce their skin.

Dasig yanked his blindfold off just in time as the eagle was about to grab his head. He ducked, and his blade met the eagle's talons, severing them. Another cry made the two humans cover their ears. Before the eagle soared upward, its talons grew back.

"Hurry! I'll distract it," Dasig shouted as he flew after the magical bird.

Every time the eagle dove in the tree's direction, Lin-ay's heart missed a beat, but she managed to reach the first branch. She stopped to catch her breath. Her legs were shaking so much that she thought she was going to fall. By the time she got to the nest, Dasig was dangling in the eagle's talons. Lin-ay grabbed the eggshell before the eagle could reach her and shoved it in her pocket.

"You didn't earn it. I'll take this man's life in return." The eagle spoke in her mind, just like Agila did.

Lin-ay leaped. Aided by her new anting-anting, her body shot upward, and she grabbed the eagle by one leg before it could fly away. With all her force, she drove her blade into the bird's body. The eagle let out a long, piercing cry. Unlike Dasig's blade, hers had been forged by Bugna, designed to kill monsters from the underworld, and the wound Lin-ay inflicted on the wild animal didn't heal. The eagle must have realized what kind of blade she was wielding, for it immediately released Dasig, who was barely conscious and just managed to slow his fall.

Lin-ay released her hold on the eagle's leg and tested her new anting-anting. She'd never flown via an anting-anting before, and her first one provided healing that she didn't need to control. This one made her feel more aware that she had it. She slowed her breathing and concentrated on the anting-anting. *Slow, slow, slow.* Her body floated in the air, just as her mind had wanted to. She landed on a branch.

"I'm sorry for taking your power," she said. "I'll make sure to put it to good use."

The eagle pecked at the remaining eggshells and gathered them together, acting like Lin-ay hadn't stolen its precious possession.

"Look, I'm sorry. Bakunawa will rise in two weeks, and I need to fly."

"I know," the animal said in a disinterested tone. Lin-ay suspected the eggshells weren't precious at all to the bird and that it only pretended to protect them. *"Now go."*

"I will pay you back. Anything, as long as it's not urgent."

"The only thing I want is to keep your mouth shut."

"Sorry."

I mean about this tree. Don't tell anyone, humans and spirits alike.

"I promise."

Lin-ay bowed and snatched a leaf then rose into the air, grateful for her newfound ability. She couldn't simply ignore the invisibility anting-anting. Just when she thought she'd escaped, twigs gripped her feet. To her horror, the tree was stretching like a human jumping to catch her. The eagle screeched, long and piercing. Lin-ay didn't need a warning. She knew she was doomed.

4

THE BOLO WARRIOR

Makanas dashed out of the kitchen as bird calls announced Dasig's return. He had made up excuses to his father to stay on the plateau since Dasig and Lin-ay left. Staying underground made him anxious, so he spent most of his time looking at the horizon. He sighed with relief at the sight of the cat Mimi flying alongside Dasig. They had succeeded in bringing the shaman along. Perhaps Putot could remove Amihan's tracker before Dungog's expected arrival of Lin-ay. As they drew closer, Makanas realized Putot rode the cat alone. "Where's Lin-ay?"

Dasig landed on the plateau with a grim expression. Putot bounced on Mimi's back as the cat's paws hit the ground. Before Makanas could ask where Lin-ay was, Dasig handed him a bamboo container, and inside was a roll of paper. Kidlat snatched it in a heartbeat. Like Makanas, Kidlat had looked up at the sky more in the last four days than they had in their entire lives.

"Bugna said you must read the letter together." Dasig bowed.

Makanas took a step closer as his father unrolled the letter.

Lin-ay is lost in the hidden tree. I peeked between the curtains of time, and the future remained the same. You must have her by your side, or you won't defeat Bakunawa. Before you journey here, stop. I can't see beyond Bakunawa's return, but I am certain humanity will survive even if you don't slay the serpent. However, if you cross the boundary between life and death, your barangay will fall into the hands of Habagat. Lin-ay needs someone she shares a connection with—someone willing to risk a life to save a life, and no, that's not Amihan. She doesn't have an anting-anting that she could bargain with the hidden tree. I'm talking about your son. I've instructed your warrior to read this letter with him so your son can decide. He must be willing or let Lin-ay perish. There is a possibility, too, that she could figure out how to escape the tree's magic on her own, but she is but a baby learning to crawl. I'm afraid it would then be too late when she returns.

Iyay could help Makanas in his spiritual journey. May the spirits and your ancestors guide you.

— SHAMAN OF SULOD

"I'm not sending my grandson into the cusp of death," Iyay huffed as she carried a charcoal cauldron into Amihan's hut, where the spaces between the walls

The Bolo Warrior

and floors were sealed with mud, ensuring Amihan couldn't see anything outside in case Dungog possessed her again. Iyay disappeared into the dark one-room hut along with Putot.

Makanas climbed the stairs to the hut and found Amihan writing on bamboo scrolls. He bowed and sat behind the two shamans. Iyay would eventually help him, he was sure, but the old woman needed some time to complain first and talk about the dangers of magic.

Putot introduced herself to Amihan and gently touched the woman's shoulder. "Ah!" Putot jerked back her hand, as if she had just touched fire. "It's not Datu Habagat's shaman. I've never felt such strong tracker magic before." She pulled a wooden stopper from a bottle and poured red powder onto the burning coals. The only lamp suffocated from smoke that swirled up from the cauldron, barely burning. "Clever. He created a mask so Amihan wouldn't feel him if he wanted to peek secretly."

"Can he use magic through her?" Iyay asked.

Putot shook her head. "Tracker magic can't do that. It's mainly for spying and forcing the victim to do something through pain. If the victim has an anting-anting, then the manipulator—in the old time, we called them puppeteers—can force the victim to use it. Some powerful ones who'd practiced this evil magic for a long time can speak through their host."

"So can you remove it?" Iyay asked.

"Hmm... Only the shaman who injected the tracker could suck it out, but in the old time, several tracker planters worked together and successfully freed the host. Let me see... We have to be careful." Putot opened her mouth in a yawn. Her body stretched and elongated as she transformed into a snake. After licking Amihan's shoulder, she transformed back into a girl. "The tracker is too strong. He could kill Amihan before I could pull it out, if I even could. I can't risk her life."

"I'm dead either way," Amihan said. "Just try it. I'd rather have that small chance of survival than put this barangay at risk."

"Your blood will be on my hands, then. As a shaman, I can't. Datu Habagat had forced me to kill so many innocent people. I know I shouldn't have but he had Mimi back then. If I let blood spill again, darkness will cloud my judgment and turn me into a monster just like him."

"So what are we going to do now?" Makanas asked.

"Follow Dungog's command."

"I will cut him into pieces myself," Iyay said that afternoon, preparing her rattan bag of bottles.

Thanks to Putot's explanation of shamans turning dark, Makanas had convinced Iyay to help him rescue Lin-ay. Though he wasn't sure if Amihan's death would count as Iyay's fault if she refused to do anything, he'd created a solid argument and assured Iyay that he'd made his spiritual journey several times through meditation.

"Mimi! It's time to go back!" Putot shouted.

The cat protested by pretending not to hear. She lay on the ground, purring softly as children petted her. Even Adlaw, who never talked to anyone, joined the kids in admiring the gigantic cat. Despite her size, Mimi's fluffiness and white fur attracted the kids quite quickly.

"Mimi, we can come back here later," Putot continued. "Bugna won't give you treats if you keep misbehaving."

Mimi finally listened and kneeled for her companion and Iyay to climb onto her back. He glided through the air as though weightless, and Makanas flew behind.

Finding Dasig's mark near the invisible tree wasn't hard. He'd bound grasses into ribbons. Had it been weeks before, the mark would have disappeared in the living forest. But Bugna's hold on the forest was weakening as Bakunawa's rising approached, and Sulod looked unremarkable, another forest free from human exploitation.

"What do I have to do?" Makanas asked. He knew where the hidden tree stood even when he couldn't see it. He gripped the hilt of the bakunawa blade, knowing that if he awakened it, he would see the tree before him. He wondered how pretty it was, that it seduced Lin-ay.

"Wait," Iyay said as she helped Putot lay some fruits on banana leaves. "Ah. Gather firewood and give me the tiger's hair."

Makanas hesitated. The tiger's hair was the last anting-anting he'd acquired before his father sent him on a mission three years before, and by far the strongest he had. But if he offered a weaker anting-anting, the hidden tree might not accept his soul. Gently, he pulled the fibers sewn around the tiger hair on his shirt.

"You'll get a stronger anting-anting later. You're a capable man," Putot said.

As they finished setting everything up, Iyay explained the difference between his meditation and the spiritual journey into the hidden tree's world. "You will appear like a dream or an illusion to Lin-ay, so be prepared. She might not believe you because she might have experienced several illusions already induced by the tree. That's why Bugna chose you, because you shared a connection with her. The hidden tree could read her past but not her feelings. Use that to your advantage. Your mission is one thing: convince her to give up the thing she stole, along with the memory of seeing this tree. If she does, her memory will be altered, and she could return to her body."

"Easy enough." Makanas shrugged as he cleared a spot near the bonfire. He lay down on the ground and closed his eyes as Iyay had instructed.

Iyay started her song. "*Tabi Tabi*, excuse these mortals for invading your peace. Let it be known by each spirit here... we have no desire to harm, nor to steal. We humbly ask your forgiveness for disturbing your peace."

Makanas wanted to see what was going on but didn't dare open his eyes. He would have to face Iyay's wrath if he didn't follow her instructions. A few moments later, he heard feet stomping the ground: Iyay and Putot dancing. The clangs of gongs followed as the two shamans chanted and offered their presents. Makanas had no idea how long he kept his eyes closed before the footsteps sounded like light taps against the soil then grew weaker and weaker until he heard nothing but silence. He rose and saw his body on the ground. He was still in the forest of Sulod, and the grasses Dasig tied into knots were still there.

He shielded his eyes against a sudden blazing yellow light. There the majestic golden tree shone like the sun, as Iyay had described. He ran toward it. As his soul touched the trunk, a door opened therein. He stepped through and looked back to mark his way, but the door disappeared. Everything felt in place. The grass was soft beneath his feet, the fluffy clouds protected him from the sun, and flowers lined the path he took.

On top of a hill, Lin-ay was combing her hair and smelling flowers. Her long, black hair swayed with the wind. Her binukot dress hugged her figure in the right places, and her beauty made him sigh.

"Lin-ay." Makanas jogged up the hill.

Lin-ay turned and smiled meekly, her eyes sparkling with joy. "You came. I've been waiting for you. What took you so long?"

"I've been waiting for you." Lin-ay would never have said that. She wouldn't want him there. She would want him to be safe.

"Who are you?" Makanas asked.

In a blink, Lin-ay disappeared, replaced by a rose leaning over another rosebush in the exact position Lin-ay had been in just moments before. He had the urge to hack the bush down, but his bakunawa blade was missing when he touched his waist. He moved on, determined to find Lin-ay. His heart missed a beat as Lin-ay reappeared, swinging a bakunawa blade. He ducked then ignored the illusion. He wondered how many fake Lin-ays he would see before finding the real her.

5

THE CHANTER

Lin-ay closed her eyes to pray to her ancestors to save her. She thought of Bulan but recoiled at the thought of the goddess controlling her body. She had to survive this as herself.

When she opened her eyes, she sensed no sound nor light and braced herself as she fell into a bottomless abyss. Something was wrong. She couldn't feel her bolo sword. She touched her waist to double check, and it was gone. Her hand immediately searched her pocket and was stunned that her healing anting-anting and the eggshell, too, were gone.

I must be dreaming... or perhaps fell hard when the tree grabbed me, and this is just a hallucination.

But it felt too real to be a dream. Then darkness gave way to blinking lights of different colors. The colors moved in a circle so quickly that her head spun. Closing her eyes didn't help. Then a loud blaring almost chased her soul from her body. It turned into a song, following the rhythm of the dizzying lights. *Stop. Stop.* Her body continued falling, and everywhere she looked, circling lights assaulted her vision. *I'm going to lose my mind.* The fall went on and on until she could no longer tell the time or which way was up or down.

Finally, she grunted as she hit the ground. The dizzying colors and sound disappeared, swallowed by warm sunlight. She knew better than to trust it came from the sun. Looking around, she found gigantic flowers. Dewdrops as big as her palms melted and sloshed down the leaves. *Have I grown smaller?* But then she noticed the bees feeding on the nectar looked normal. Lin-ay looked up, expecting a gaping hole she could climb up, but all she could see was the blue sky decorated with fluffy clouds.

Her heart skipped a beat as a snake crawled past a few paces away, leaving behind eggshells pulsing with immeasurable power. She dashed to steal one, ignoring a warning in her mind that the snake would strike her. Before she could reach the shell, another anting-anting in the form of a lion's hair appeared ahead, brighter, and demanded her attention.

She cursed herself for falling into the illusion. Even if the anting-antings were indeed real, she was in the magical tree's territory, where things didn't make sense. She had to convince herself the place wasn't real. That might help her get out, but no matter how many times she whispered that she was dreaming, she couldn't see Sulod. She straightened, preparing herself to fly, but she remained on the ground. Even the new power she'd gotten didn't work. She had to do something.

"Forgive my actions," Lin-ay said, convinced that the tree could hear and sense her.

She bowed low, the lowest she could to anyone of authority. She had to choose her words carefully. One thing she'd learned from her mother and the traitor Dungog, is that a word is sometimes more powerful than swords, if wielded correctly.

"I know I should've asked permission, and I was wrong to take something I do not deserve. It was a desperate act done due to my impulsive nature, one I deeply regret." She kept her head low, waiting for any change. "Bakunawa will rise, and Bugna has foretold I'm the only one who can defeat it."

A slight shift in the air made her want to look.

Not yet. And now for the finale. "I will give back what I took and pay for my actions with anything you deem necessary."

A crow cawed, urgent, and Lin-ay looked up. She followed it and gasped as the crow perched on the golden tree, exactly the same tree that had caught her and brought her there.

The crow cawed again, but that time, Lin-ay could understand it: *"Return the leaf where it belongs. If you make a mistake, I will take your life."*

"But I don't have it."

Her hand automatically fished in her pocket to prove herself to the crow, and she found the leaf in her pocket, golden and pulsing with power. *This is easy.* She knew which branch she'd plucked it from. Groaning with effort, she pulled herself up to the first branch. *No, higher.* She remembered looking down at the eagle when she plucked the leaf. Her climb got easier as the higher branches were closer to each other. She had to stop, for she didn't know exactly which branch she had rested on. She resorted instead to checking twigs that were missing leaves, but she found too many. *Why can't I remember which branch? And why are there too many missing leaves?*

"It's not this tree." She came to the conclusion as the words escaped her mouth.

"Clever," the crow said. *"At least you paid attention before you stole it."*

Rage boiled within her. She had no time to waste. *The tree should just accept the leaf!* But she couldn't lose her patience. If she angered the tree, she might get trapped forever. She climbed down, determined to return the leaf to its rightful place, but when she reached the ground, two dozen trees greeted her, exactly alike. She wouldn't finish in a day and didn't know what else the tree would do to her after that challenge. She wouldn't play its game.

But what can I do? I have no weapon or anting-anting. She wished she was Una, who seemed to solve all her problems with anger, or perhaps Makanas, strong, brave, and strategic. She could call Bulan, but the goddess terrified her more than the tree. *No. I am the goddess,* she convinced herself. But if she called the spirit right then, it might occupy her body instead of trying to merge with her soul. *What if I can't get back after the spirit entered my body?* Having the power of Bulan's spirit didn't guarantee her mother's freedom. Bulan didn't seem to be bothered by earthly affairs, perhaps because she was purely a goddess. Lin-ay had nothing to offer to the tree—nothing but... *my life.*

"Take my life instead." *Dear spirits, I hope this works.* "If this one leaf equals the chance of saving the world from Bakunawa, then so be it. But you should know that if I die, the bakunawa blades will fall into the hands of Dungog and Habagat. And you won't be able to hide from them either. If my action was too appalling for you to look away, then punish me."

Thinking she must sound pathetic, like a child making senseless threats, she opened her hand and let the leaf fall to the ground. At any moment, the tree would claim her. If she disappeared, Dungog would know, and perhaps he wouldn't threaten to hurt Amihan anymore.

But the leaf floated in the air. It rose and swayed toward the golden tree, suddenly the only one left. But when it got closer, the wind blew it back, and it landed in Lin-ay's pocket.

"Take it back! I don't want it. Take your stupid magic back!" Lin-ay screamed as she found herself falling again. She slammed to the ground then gasped and opened her eyes.

Golden leaves greeted her, and the eagle was looking down and spread its wings as though relieved to see her. *Is this another test?* When she sat up, it occurred to her that Sulod was no longer quiet. She turned and saw Iyay and Putot dancing. Iyay was panting, and her blouse was soaked in sweat.

Lin-ay fished in her pocket and confirmed that the leaf was indeed there. She had to return it. She would have to find a way to get another anting-anting to fly.

"*It's yours,*" the eagle said. "*The tree deemed you worthy of it, for knowing how to bargain.*"

Lin-ay dipped her head in shame. She didn't deserve it. She had to insist the tree take it back. But before she could start her climb, Iyay's horrified voice made her heart race.

"Return! You must return now, or you'll die!"

Lin-ay raced toward the bonfire as she spotted Makanas on the ground. "What happened to him?"

The two shamans gave her a brief look then returned to their dancing and chanting. Desperation blazed in Iyay's eyes. Lin-ay realized she'd heard the chant before, back when she was young, when Dungog had to call back a soul who had departed from a body, to raise the person from the dead.

"Makanas, wake up." Lin-ay knelt and pressed the ylang-ylang anting-anting to his belly button, which was believed to have a connection to a person's soul. "The barangay needs you."

Makanas bolted up, eyes wide. "Lin-ay. How did you escape?"

Iyay slouched, sweat trickling down her brow. "Didn't I tell you to return when you feel the tug?" She twisted Makanas's ear as if he was still a child.

The Bolo Warrior

"I couldn't even if I wanted to. How long was I there?" He looked up at the sky.

"We have two days left." Iyay settled into a cross-legged position on the ground.

"I've been there for five days?" Lin-ay felt like she had been inside the tree for less than an hour. "Then I have to go and see Dungog."

"No!" Makanas and Iyay shouted.

"So did Putot remove the tracker?"

Putot shook her head. The shaman who looked like a child rested a hand against a tree to support herself, looking as exhausted as Iyay.

Lin-ay gripped the hilt of her bolo blade. "I hate to do this, but I have no choice. If you try to stop me, we would have to fight."

"Lin-ay, you're not thinking straight. Even though she's your mother, think of the many lives we'll lose if you choose to save her," Putot said in her high-pitched voice.

Lin-ay hated to think about it because Putot was right. But Lin-ay might be able to escape Dungog. "Tell Head Warrior Kidlat I will be back in two days. Be it as Lin-ay or Bulan, I will be back." She turned to go.

"There is a way!" Makanas shouted. "There's a place where your mother can hide... without magic, just like Datu Habagat's underground."

Lin-ay whirled. "Why didn't you tell me sooner?"

"Because my father might not agree. The place is inside the plateau, where our weapons and warriors are positioned. If Dungog sees that..." Makanas shook his head, as if trying not to even think of the possibility. "But since Dungog can't use his magic, we could cover your mother's eyes while moving her there. But first, we have to convince my father to let Amihan into that room."

Lin-ay paced, mind racing. A big part of her was shouting that she must listen to Makanas. After all, Kidlat was better than Dungog. But she knew Kidlat lacked empathy and might choose to let Amihan die rather than let her into the warriors' hideout. She had two days left. *Two days*. She cursed herself for wasting time with the tree's anting-anting.

"He'll listen to me," Iyay said as she rose. She gathered her bag and put out the bonfire. "Now, let's go home."

"No," was Kidlat's firm answer when Iyay proposed the solution.

"Then I have no choice but to go," Lin-ay said in an equally firm voice.

After about half a day of heated argument between Iyay and Kidlat, the head warrior gave in, just as Iyay had expected. Amihan was blindfolded several times, and her hands were tied to prevent her from touching anything before she was moved to her new quarters.

The following morning, Lin-ay prepared food and fresh clothes for Amihan. She also brought needles and plain clothes for embroidery, hoping that would occupy Amihan's mind and chase boredom away. Despite the possible doom of the world, her heart felt light. She silently thanked the good spirits for keeping her mother and brother safe from Dungog, regardless if it was for only a week or a day. She smiled and greeted everyone she met along the stairs as she walked through the underground. She passed Head Guard Uwak's station with quiet footsteps. She was planning to see him after visiting her mother. Bakunawa was going to rise in about a week, but she'd tried sensing anting-antings in the air only once.

Makanas waited outside Amihan's cell, holding one of the bright orbs. His face brightened just like the light when they locked eyes. He unlocked the door and held out the orb. "I'll carry all that for you. You hold the light."

"It's fine. They're not heavy," Lin-ay said, avoiding his eyes. They had never been alone for a long time, and she seemed to forget how to speak to him without talking about the Bakunawa's rising or saving her mother.

"It's a bit far, and the passageway is narrow." Makanas placed the glowing orb on the ground and reached for Lin-ay's bags. His hand brushed against hers.

Flustered, Lin-ay let her hand drop and picked up the orb. "The light is weaker."

Makanas set Amihan's items on the ground and leaned closer to the orb. "Find the small hole," he rotated the orb on Lin-ay's hand, "and cover it with a finger."

Lin-ay's mind seemed to have frozen. She heard Makanas but wasn't processing his words. His closeness was overwhelming. Instead of trying to find the opening of the orb, he covered her hands with his. Under the soft light, she dared look up at him and met his tender gaze. They stared at each other for an eternity. If a love spell existed, it couldn't have been stronger than what she was under, for she rose to her tiptoes without even realizing it and pressed her lips against his. His arm circled her waist, pulling her even closer.

"You must come untainted."

Lin-ay pulled back as though doused by a bucket of water. Dungog's words had come unbidden.

Can he see the future like Bugna? Was that why he said those words? "I-I found it." She pressed a finger against a tiny hole, causing the passage to brighten.

She followed the zigzag pattern until they finally reached a dead end. The room was buried so deep in the mountain that, despite the gaps between the iron bars, a prisoner couldn't see anything past the wall facing the door. On the wall was another orb, glowing faintly. At first, Lin-ay thought Amihan had escaped, but her mother stirred and sat up from a mat as the increased light hit her face. She had grown so thin that she almost disappeared under the blanket. The chains rattled as Makanas unlocked the bar.

"You have two days left, Binukot." Amihan was on

her knees, eyes shining with malice as she stared at Lin-ay. "As punishment for disobeying me, I'll let you hear Amihan's screams for two days. But don't worry—I won't kill her. Not yet. But if you don't get here by midnight of the seventh day..." Dungog didn't need to complete his sentence.

"Open it," she told Makanas. She needed to know if Makanas and Kidlat had lied about the room. If Makanas had, she wouldn't forgive him.

"He's dangerous."

"Open it."

Makanas opened the door and followed Lin-ay inside. He hadn't lied. The moment she stepped inside, she tried to fly but couldn't. Taking a deep breath, she tried to sense the golden leaf, the eagle's eggshell, and the ylang-ylang flower, but she failed.

"Didn't Kidlat tell you his concealer was from Datu Bangkaw?" Dungog asked, eyes glued to Makanas. Dungog clucked his tongue. "And you didn't even question why Datu Bangkaw's anting-anting worked while the rest of yours failed. You're just like your father, arrogant. Fool. You two think you have everything figured out." Amihan turned to Lin-ay. "If I were you, Binukot, I would make use of my remaining time convincing my lover to fly me here."

He doesn't know that I have a new anting-anting, or perhaps that's what he wants me to think. "And live as your slave forever? I'd rather not exist at all." Lin-ay hated that Dungog was speaking through her mother, so she turned and left.

Makanas grabbed her arm. "Don't tell me you'll do as Dungog wants. He'll have two hostages if you meet him."

"I have no choice but to face what is now."

"He asked Datu Habagat to heal Amihan before. He won't kill your mother."

"I hope, but we're not sure, and I can't gamble with my mother's life." Lin-ay raced up the stairs, ignoring Makanas's pleading. "Tell your father I'm sorry. No matter what happens, I'll try to get back here when Bakunawa rises."

"You're staying," Kidlat said from up above. Behind him were Una, Dasig, and more warriors blocking her path.

Una came down the stairs and held Lin-ay's hand tightly. "I'm sorry," she whispered, not meeting her eyes.

Dasig held her other hand, and another warrior untied the sword from her waist. Lin-ay sought Makanas's eyes. His face contorted with mixed emotions.

"You can't do this," Lin-ay protested.

"I must," Kidlat answered. "Bugna said you must be here when Bakunawa rises. She didn't say whether as a warrior or a prisoner."

The distinctive ring of a blade shattered Lin-ay's concentration.

Kidlat shot forward and slapped Makanas, whose blade fell back into its sheath. "Weak. That's why you're never going to be the head warrior."

Makanas's face flushed red with anger. He kept his head high and defiant, unlike before. Lin-ay wanted to lash out, to berate Kidlat for hitting his son in front of other warriors, but at that moment, she wondered if the head warrior even loved his son. When Una ushered her back to Amihan's cell, Lin-ay walked without resisting. She needed to find a way to escape. Lashing out wouldn't work. She would only waste her time and energy. Una gently pushed her into Amihan's cell. Lin-ay expected the woman to say something, perhaps to hurl sharp words as she always did or blame Lin-ay for not seeing the whole picture, but the warrior was looking anywhere but at her.

Lin-ay finally decided what to say. "Una, tell Inday to take care of Adlaw."

"The boy's safe." Una turned toward the door. "He'll probably pass by here tomorrow before they move to the—"

"Stop!" Lin-ay shouted. "You must tell Kidlat the concealer doesn't work on Dungog."

"Just as he had suspected." Una sighed. "I know you hate the head warrior now and maybe all of us, but I hope that when all of this is over, we can fight together rather than against each other."

Lin-ay's tears threatened to fall as Una's lazy footsteps disappeared. She squared her shoulders, focusing on finding a solution. No one would dare to free her. Perhaps Makanas would try, but with Bakunawa's rising upon them, Kidlat might have already convinced him to turn a blind eye. Her heart raced at the memory of their kiss. She prayed they could be together in the future but then pushed the thought aside. She had to focus on saving her mother.

Inday might try to fight her way into the cell, but Lin-ay was sure Kidlat had already stopped any possibility of her getting near. She looked around for something to pick the lock. She herself had told legends of great warriors escaping captivity and chanted about heroes on the brink of death only to come out stronger when the audience least expected it. She had to try. She was Bulan, the goddess of war and the hero of chants, whom even the gods of the *pangayaw* colonizers had failed to crush. She closed her eyes and welcomed her spirit, praying even though she knew she herself was Bulan. She begged for the spirit to come, but all she could hear was Amihan's faint breath, breath that could stop at any moment if Dungog decided Lin-ay wouldn't play his game.

Lin-ay opened her eyes. Amihan lay still, crumpled on the ground in her dirty clothes. Lin-ay didn't want to wake her up and stare into Dungog's eyes. She rummaged through the clothing she and Makanas had brought in earlier, hoping for a hair pin or perhaps a needle that a girl had absentmindedly left when altering the dresses to match Amihan's size, but she found none.

"Thank the spirits you're still here," Amihan said in a weak voice. She sat up and, with shaky hands, tried to smooth her hair.

"Help me, Mother." Lin-ay hurriedly explained how Kidlat had imprisoned her.

Amihan reached out to a bundle of roasted sweet potato and ate. "It was a difficult decision to make, but I would've done the same."

"I don't want you to die."

"You're old enough to take care of your brother. I just want to be with your father in the afterlife."

"Mother!" Lin-ay expected Amihan to threaten her with punishment for raising her voice, but then she realized they were both imprisoned, and no punishment could be worse than not being able to do anything. "I'll try to call Bulan again."

"Not now," Amihan said, her face calm. "Kidlat will need you to merge with your spirit when Bakunawa rises. Each time you use your power, your connection becomes stronger, but you must do so under Bugna's supervision. She's studied this for a thousand years."

However, her only chance of escaping was Bulan, the goddess she was terrified of. She felt the tip of the bakunawa blade in her pocket, but she couldn't sense the power in anything. Even the hidden tree's leaf felt just like an ordinary object.

"Dungog," Lin-ay called.

Wide-eyed, Amihan looked at her. "Dear spirits, what are you thinking?"

"I know you're in there. And I know you're dying to meet me. How about you teach me how to defeat the concealer?"

"Clever," Amihan smiled Dungog's crooked smile.

"I wondered how long it'd take for you to figure it out. You proved to be smarter than Kidlat's son." Amihan's teeth sank into her finger until blood ran down her cheeks. "Come closer, dear." Amihan cupped Lin-ay's face, smearing blood on it. "See you soon."

6

THE BOLO WARRIOR

Waiting was the hardest part, Iyay had said. Makanas wished that were true. He hoped waiting and preparing was the worst of all and they could defeat Bakunawa and Datu Habagat as easily as they had projected. Kidlat, on the other hand, always assumed the worst, and no matter how many times they made sure every detail was as planned, he continued to force Makanas to be thorough.

He couldn't steer his mind away from Lin-ay and the kiss they'd shared. Dread filled him with each moment she shared with her mother. *What if Dungog kills her through Amihan?* He knew the thought was beyond reason because Dungog needed Lin-ay alive, but he couldn't stop himself from thinking of all the danger Lin-ay was in. He didn't want to lose her, either to Dungog or Bulan. He didn't want the goddess spirit to take over her body because Lin-ay would lose her feelings for him.

When he almost bumped against a flying warrior, he shook his head to focus. He hadn't noticed he'd been flying in the wrong direction.

The fog had descended, blanketing the mountains in white. Cold wind seeped through his bones as he flew to the north. He was performing his last check for the day, making sure the rocks were in place and wouldn't roll down the narrow pass before the day when Datu Habagat and Dungog's warriors marched in. The trap wouldn't take care of any flying warriors, but Kidlat suspected most of the enemies couldn't fly anyway.

Makanas put both hands against his lips and whistled a bird's call. A warrior answered his greeting from up the steep slope. Before he could land, a piercing call from Una echoed through the mountains. He relayed the message, and the mountains echoed with bird calls.

How did Lin-ay escape? She couldn't have gone far unless she had help. She couldn't fly, unless she called her spirit, which she was terrified of. He flew back toward the Bolo Warrior Barangay. She wouldn't have taken the usual route down the river. That would have been too obvious, but she didn't know the path to the new refuge. He headed south and whistled, letting other warriors know he hadn't found her. He needed a witness. He flew up to the plateau and entered the underground.

Kidlat was faster than he. The head warrior knelt on one knee, meeting Amihan eye to eye. "How did she escape?"

"Why, I helped her, of course." Dungog said in

Amihan's voice. "Perhaps you can go after her. She took the east route, but you better be careful. When her memory returns, she'll kill you first."

East. Makanas exited quietly. Chains rattled as Kidlat locked the prison cell and flew past Makanas. Makanas followed his father toward the east sea. A few warriors flew behind them. In the dark night, a round, mellow light that looked like the moon hovered over the sea, and Kidlat headed toward it. It wasn't the moon but Lin-ay glowing.

Kidlat dipped his head. "Oh, great warrior goddess, we are humbled in your presence."

Lin-ay glanced at Kidlat then up at the sky. "This body wants to go somewhere. It's pestering me to visit this Dungog human. I just wanted to wait for the full moon."

Still bent to his waist, Kidlat replied, "There's no better place to wait than our barangay. If you please, follow me back to the plateau."

"Lin-ay," Makanas called gently.

Lin-ay's gaze bored through him.

"Warrior," Kidlat warned.

"Lin-ay. Save your mother," Makanas said more loudly. "Save yourself."

Lin-ay frowned. For a moment, Makanas knew Lin-ay was struggling to gain control.

"Enough!" Kidlat roared and backhanded Makanas.

Lin-ay shot Kidlat a fiery look. Lightning without thunder hit Kidlat, and he plummeted down to the sea.

Warriors dove to catch him, while Makanas sped up after Lin-ay. She flew faster than anyone he'd seen.

"Lin-ay! You must return. You must not surrender to Bulan!"

He was too late. The light went out, and Lin-ay was no longer in sight.

Kidlat rose, an angry lightning scar decorating his face. "You have a knack for ruining things. After Bakunawa's rising, it would be best for you to leave the barangay. Tonight, you only proved that you're not fit to be a warrior and the barangay isn't your priority."

Makanas clenched his fists. This was the harshest proclamation his father had made. *But why after Bakunawa's rising? Why didn't he simply kick me out? Is he hoping I will redeem myself? What would he do if I just leave now? Would he go after me like he had tried with Lin-ay? Maybe not, because no prophecy says I could defeat Bakunawa.* For a moment, Makanas was tempted to leave. He was strong enough to be on his own. But all he knew was being a warrior. Without his position, he would have no purpose in living. And without Kidlat's help, he couldn't kill Datu Habagat and avenge his mother. He had to endure the humiliation. When Bakunawa rose, he would kill Datu Habagat and perhaps leave the barangay with Lin-ay.

Bugna appeared out of nowhere with Putot riding her white cat, shattering the heavy air between Makanas and Kidlat. "You'll have to fight me if you're thinking of leaving the barangay," Bugna said. "You can't control the goddess. Return to your barangay."

"There's no point in preparing if Habagat gets Bulan!" Kidlat gripped his blade, knuckles white. "I might as well cut their heads off first."

"Send your son instead."

Kidlat whirled, lips thin with anger. "He just proved useless tonight. I'm tired of your prophecy. This child has no common sense."

"He was the only one pulling Lin-ay out of the surface, you fool!" Bugna's voice thundered. "You need the girl to merge with the spirit to become the Bulan that we need."

"I just need the goddess to kill Bakunawa, whole or just the spirit."

"And what if she sends Bakunawa back to the underworld? Your son has given you a greater advantage by bringing you the girl, but you managed to lose her. Send your son to Dungog. He won't kill him. By now, he knows the boy could call forth Lin-ay. Better to lock the goddess out of her reach than have Dungog use her."

"He's weak."

"He's human with emotions." Bugna beckoned Makanas, who glided toward her. She raised an eyebrow as Kidlat turned his back without paying any respect. "You might die in this attempt," she told Makanas.

"It doesn't matter," he said. "But since when did you see Lin-ay as the most important person for defeating Bakunawa? Father didn't send me to get her."

"When you brought her to Sulod the first time." In

another breath, they reached Sulod and landed in front of Bugna's stone house. "Dungog and Habagat might use you to distract Kidlat."

"I'd rather lose my life before then." Makanas bowed and alighted.

Suddenly, a demon was barreling down upon them from the east. It looked like a man, save for its horns, red eyes, and mountainous size. Makanas unsheathed his bakunawa blade. As he blazed toward the demon, it ran to meet him at equal speed. Red light shot from its eyes, burning everything on the way. Makanas soared upward to dodge.

"Dear spirits, Bugna! Help me."

When he turned, Bugna was nowhere to be seen. In that brief moment of distraction, the demon grabbed his leg and pulled him down to the ground. Makanas slashed, barely missing his own leg. The demon's severed hand still clung to his leg, and he hacked it with the back of his sword. As its grasp came undone, the demon's arm healed, its hand growing back at impossible speed. He needed someone to distract the demon. *Lin-ay*. With her strong healing anting-anting, Lin-ay had been perfect at being the bait. He should've been looking for her then, but there he was, fighting an afterlife runaway that should be Bugna's responsibility. He had to kill it quickly. The longer he spent there, the stronger Bulan would become.

The demon jumped and tried to stomp on Makanas. Makanas dodged in what seemed like a dance. With Makanas fighting on the ground, the demon seemed to favor its legs. Makanas tested his theory. He flew up and then dove. The demon couldn't bend nor look down. That was why it was trying to stomp on Makanas. In quick succession, he slashed the demon's legs. They grew back, but not quickly enough, and the demon steadily became shorter. When Makanas was about to cut the remaining thigh, he gasped as his feet were lifted into the air. A gigantic hand circled his throat.

The demon's mouth cracked open, revealing pointy black teeth. "Tasty."

The demon's grip was too tight, and Makanas's vision blurred. His brain told him to shout for Bugna, if only he could speak. He couldn't die. He needed to save Lin-ay. Dimly aware of the blade in his hand, he prayed. He had never prayed before.

Bulan, great warrior who forged this sword, forgive this unworthy warrior who dares call your name. You have promised to protect your people. Oh, please look upon this humble warrior and grace me with your power… to save lives.

When Makanas opened his eyes, he saw nothing but darkness. For a moment, he thought he was dead, but then a blinding light appeared out of nowhere. In the center was a girl floating in the air. Her straight hair traced down her back like a waterfall in sharp contrast to her soft, immaculate dress. She looked so fragile and familiar. The girl hummed, moving her body in an elegant dance.

Makanas thought he'd heard that voice before. "Lin-ay?"

The girl turned but seemed not to see him. Makanas saw a blade just beneath the girl's feet that he thought hadn't been there before. As the girl started another song, the blade separated into seven smaller swords. That wasn't Lin-ay. She was Bulan.

His surroundings shifted. When he looked down, a serpent shot up, openmouthed. Makanas wanted to fly, to flee from Bakunawa, but he couldn't see his own body. Seven blades surrounded Bakunawa, locking the serpent in place and stopping its flight toward the moon. This Bakunawa was very different from what his father had described. It was indeed gigantic, but it didn't look like it was rising to bring terror, perhaps because of the seven blades surrounding it. Bakunawa's face was serene, almost like Bulan. And when the seven blades slowly backed away, the serpent dove quietly back into the ocean.

Makanas gasped and found himself breathing again and still fighting the demon. In the corner of his vision, a soft purple glow danced and swirled. Power surged from the blade, complementing his anting-anting. His kick landed right in the demon's chest, followed by the bakunawa blade slashing right through its body. Makanas didn't stop until the demon was cut in half from the head down to its bottom.

"I have awakened the blade." His voice trembled.

PART II

"Banishment!" The gods and goddesses chanted. The word roared like a tidal wave against the walls.

Bathala's piercing gaze bore through the crowd. The supreme ruler of the gods held up a hand. The gods' and goddesses' mouths opened and closed in protest, but the words lodged in their throats, for Bathala needed them to listen.

"These two were banished a long time ago," he said. "Banishment isn't a punishment for them."

Bulan dared look up at her father. "You can banish us forever."

"You side with the humans," Bathala roared, "and now you want your punishment to be with them forever!"

Bulan side-eyed Bakunawa, wanting him to say something. The two of them, after all, had led other demigods to side with the humans in the revolution against the gods. But he was remaining quiet, having said only that he would accept whatever punishment the council imposed.

Some gods had proposed obliteration, but Bathala shut that idea down. The gods were growing more anxious the longer Bulan and Bakunawa remained in the realm, and they were afraid Bathala would simply forgive them. Bulan knew the gods would rather have them banished because their presence reminded them of Bulan and Bakunawa's treachery.

"Strip them of their humanity!" Dilim, the god of the afterlife and chaos stood, spreading his dark aura among the gods. Murmurs traveled from ear to ear like the swirling smoke blanketing the white floor. No one dared to oppose him or to side with him openly.

Bathala cleared the air with a wave of his hand. "And how do you suggest we do that?"

Bakunawa stilled. Bulan's human heart drummed. Never in known history had a demigod been stripped of its humanity. That would be like killing the god itself. Bulan wanted to protest, but she protected the fear inside herself, masking it with an indifferent resolve to accept whatever the punishment was.

"That's an abomination!" Ganda, Bulan's mortal mother and Bathala's wife, knocked her staff against the white floor. "Being half human made them stronger, not in the ways gods see. Because of them, all of you saw how cruel you could be. You saw reason!" Despite her loud voice, Ganda was ignored by the gods, as always.

Her beauty might capture the iciest heart of any man on earth, but in the gods' realm, where beauty could be bent in a blink, Ganda caught only Bathala's eyes and no one else's.

"What makes them human? Greed and emotion." Dilim stood again, his dark aura weaker but always on the surface, ready to spread. "Better to get rid of them."

Ganda forced a laugh. "Oh, Dilim. Don't think of yourself so high and mighty. Your greed is greater than any human's."

Dilim shrugged, dismissing Ganda's words. "I suggest splitting their human souls from their spirits."

"They would only rejoin with their human forms once reborn." Bathala shook his head gently.

"Not if we erase their memories."

Bulan clenched her fist tightly. Her memories had been erased before. It wasn't a pleasant experience. Even then, she was still a god with all her powers. She wondered what would happen to her human body if she was reborn as a helpless human.

"For how many human lives do you suggest?" Bathala slowly looked around at the gods beneath him.

"Until they learn their lesson!" Dilim grinned.

7
THE CHANTER

Lin-ay heard Makanas's voice clearly, as though he was next to her. Lin-ay wanted to turn, to make sure Makanas was fine, but Bulan was controlling her body. She could feel the spirit listening to Makanas, its grip loosening. She pushed the spirit out as though the goddess was a physical entity.

Lin-ay's heart felt like it would leap out of her chest as she suddenly plummeted toward the sea. Her spirit had ejected from her body so suddenly that, for a moment, she forgot how to move on her own. Before she hit the ocean, she remembered she had an anting-anting with the power of flight.

"I am Lin-ay. I am Lin-ay. I am Lin-ay," she repeated the words like a prayer.

She could feel the broken tip of the bakunawa blade in her pocket but felt like her old self. She had regained her lost memories, from the most recent reincarnations up to when she had been Bugna's daughter. If her spirit had stayed inside her for a longer time, she might have regained all the memories but perhaps lost her humanity.

The dark sky speckled with stars wasn't enough to give her directions. The occasional disturbance in the water told her only what she already knew—she was too far to the east. She closed her eyes, trying to remember the hand-drawn map she'd studied with her mother when she was ten. The eastern sea extended past Sulod, and to the north was the Kadamuan city. She needed to get back to the west before going north to her own barangay. She wished she had real-life experience at reading the stars, but sailing had never been meant for a binukot.

Without an idea of her direction, Lin-ay turned and flew, hoping she was heading west. The time must have been midnight, and even if she lost a night wandering, she could still reach Dungog's barangay—her father's former barangay in a day with her new ability to fly. As she flew in the dark, she wondered why Bulan had been so bent on getting to the east. As far as Lin-ay knew, the gate to the underworld was near Sulod.

Stars sparkled to her left. *Strange. I can't possibly be flying among the stars.* Curious, Lin-ay followed them. A moment later, she realized they weren't stars but fireflies. As Lin-ay drew closer, they gathered to form a ball of light. Lin-ay remembered the first time she'd passed by Sulod. *Are they the same fireflies? How did they know I'm here?* As fireflies had helped her before, she trusted them, and after what seemed like an endless flight in the cold night, she saw the white shoreline. She was near Sulod.

The sun was rising by the time she reached Dungog's barangay. Her heart ached at the sight of their old house, torn to shreds, just like her father. She didn't even bother hiding her anting-antings. She wiped her tears and glided toward Dungog's house. The two-story bamboo house was swarmed with armed men. Dungog must have expected an epic fight. She noted the extended veranda, the new kitchen roof, and the fresh logs beside the house. If he had amassed great wealth from betraying his former datu, he would have prepared a stone house. Lin-ay wondered if he had fully comprehended the amount of tax the pangayaw colonizers required from barangays. He would have to bleed his people dry to live in luxury.

When she landed before the stairs, Dungog's warriors surrounded her and tied her hands at her back. They let her climb on her own, but their spears followed her. The stairs led to the veranda, where Dungog sat cross legged. Lin-ay sat opposite him.

"*Salabat.*" Dungog pushed a porcelain cup gently toward Lin-ay. He had the decency to serve her warm ginger tea with honey, as though he knew she'd been out in the sea, cold and hungry. He bowed slightly, as if they were friends just about to have a chat.

Lin-ay shrugged her shoulders.

Dungog nodded to a warrior behind Lin-ay and the warrior untied her hands. He waved a hand and the warriors backed away.

Lin-ay grabbed the cup with both hands, grateful for the warmth. Ignoring the warning of poison in her mind, she sipped slowly, savoring the aroma. She didn't think she needed to worry about poison since Dungog himself was like a venom that corrupted her mind.

"Thank you," she managed to say.

Dungog raised an eyebrow, perhaps wondering if Lin-ay had forgotten he was the reason for her father's death. "I'd expected to meet Bulan." He raised both hands and looked down at his trousers, pinned with all sorts of anting-antings. "How did you manage to banish her?"

"I didn't."

Dungog smirked as if to say, *"Don't lie to me."*

"Someone prayed fervently, and the goddess had to answer."

Dungog's mouth relaxed, and Lin-ay was glad he didn't laugh. She couldn't seem to erase the memory of her mother with Dungog's wheezing laugh.

"Why, of course, she's half human."

Lin-ay realized then that Dungog didn't know that Lin-ay herself was Bulan. Somehow, his knowledge of Bulan's rebirth was tainted. She would think hard on how to use Dungog's ignorance, but for the moment, the ache in her muscles dulled. Her worries faded like the harsh sunlight blocked by a thick curtain. When her eyes started to close, she didn't care that Dungog smiled in triumph.

When she came to, she lay on a straw mat in a dark stone room similar to her mother's prison. She had no doubt it was sealed with a concealer magic. Her hands were free and her mind clear.

Dungog came into Lin-ay's view from the corner of the room. "I need you to be free from Bulan for a week." He sat cross-legged and caressed a fist-sized round stone. It was as dark as the stone Datu Habagat had used to trap Mimi.

"Suit yourself. I don't care. You're going to lose anyway."

"Why? What makes you that confident? I'm sure Bugna told Kidlat you're his most powerful weapon. You're planning to betray me, aren't you?"

Lin-ay laughed. "I don't even know what to do. Everyone's telling me to control this goddess, but I guess all of you are just as clueless as I am. You have no idea how strong she is."

"But you banished her."

"By chance. Lucky some idiot deserved her attention at that moment."

"Exactly. Now all we need to do is find that idiot. I have an idea you know exactly who it is."

Lin-ay wanted to ask Dungog what he meant, but fear muted her words. She berated herself for being too careless with her words.

"Let me guess..." Dungog continued. "Kidlat? No." He shook his head slowly. "He's not the type to appeal to emotion. His son, then."

Lin-ay wished she had a mask to hide her face or had been trained how to lie. She swallowed hard, praying that Kidlat had done a good job of keeping Makanas in the barangay.

"It doesn't matter. We'll worry about that." His gaze flicked between her and the stone he was holding. "Has Kidlat shown you anything like this?" When Lin-ay didn't answer, he shrugged. "Well, he was probably going to show it to you at the very last moment, but I—a meticulous man—want everything planned ahead. When you kill Bakunawa, this snare ball will suck its soul and power."

Snare ball. To Lin-ay, the name sounded ridiculous, like it was meant to trap animals. "You do it. I have no clue how."

"Fortunately, you don't have to do anything. It'll suck the soul of any magical creature near it."

Lin-ay held out a hand. "Fine. I'll do it. Just remove your tracker now."

"Oh, no, dear. You seem to forget what I said. I told you I would've killed your mother if you didn't come here. I never said anything about removing the tracker, but I will after you slay Bakunawa." Dungog tilted his head as though listening to something Lin-ay couldn't hear. "See you later, dear."

The stone door closed, leaving Lin-ay alone and cold. She pressed her hand against her pocket, feeling the tip of the bakunawa blade smeared with Amihan's blood. She didn't dare touch it. Hoping the blood would neutralize the concealer, she had coated the blade with it when she escaped her mother's cell. Dungog, like Kidlat, might have been able to sense anting-anting, but he hadn't confiscated Lin-ay's. Perhaps he was overconfident about the concealer suppressing their powers. Even when they didn't work, they brought comfort to Lin-ay, and she found herself tracing every vein of the leaf of the hidden tree as she took it from her pocket.

"Bulan..." Lin-ay dared to call, but just as she had expected, she couldn't feel her spirit. She gave in to sleep, and when she woke up from the cold wind, she felt like she had just the most restful sleep in a very long time. Dungog had returned. Before the door closed, she noted it was already dark outside. She had slept the whole afternoon. If Makanas wasn't here yet, then he must have decided not to follow her.

Dungog held a lamp, illuminating the scarred body of a man next to him. Lin-ay sat straight to present herself well, a habit when facing someone, and looked up into the face of the cruel man she'd met before—Datu Habagat.

Datu Habagat crouched and examined her face. "I can't believe I just let you go last time." His hand reached out to touch her face.

Lin-ay was revolted by his touch. She wanted to slap his hand away but gritted her teeth and kept as still as a statue.

"So this is the goddess's face. What a shame. I could've proposed a marriage when you were still a binukot. The outside world has tainted your beauty."

"It is no matter," Dungog said sharply.

"Right." Datu Bangkaw stood. "Forgive my worldly

feelings, Datu Dungog." He turned toward the door. "Come forth."

A boy stepped forward, his eyes as dark and round as Putot's. He stretched as though about to yawn and transformed into a snake.

"No." Lin-ay whimpered.

They were going to put a tracker on her. But before the snake could strike, it transformed into a boy again, backing away quickly. Fear made his eyes even bigger. "I can't. She's already being tracked by someone more powerful."

"Who?" Datu Dungog and Datu Habagat chorused.

"A goddess."

8

THE BOLO WARRIOR

"Well done, young man. And you did it with your first real fight with the blade." Bugna glided toward Makanas.

"Why didn't you tell me how to awaken the blade before?" Makanas couldn't help but wonder at the soft light emitted by the blade. Stronger than any anting-anting he'd had, the blade seemed to slowly unite with his shivering body. His senses heightened, and the anting-antings' power seemed to double in strength.

"You had no one to protect before, and all you thought about was revenge."

"Did I waste all my youth in useless training then? Why didn't you tell my father before?" He wanted to fly right away to find Lin-ay, but he needed answers.

Bugna shook her head. "With your sword skills, you'll be one with the blade in no time. That, at least, Kidlat was successful at, but don't be overconfident. Habagat, too, had awakened the blade."

Bugna tilted her head, and her unfocused eyes darkened. Makanas called her name, but the shaman seemed to be in another place, looking past what was in front of her. She screamed, her voice echoing in the enchanted forest. Makanas crossed the distance between them as she fell to the ground.

"Bugna! What is it?"

The shaman shook her head slightly, as if that took all her effort. Makanas sheathed his bakunawa blade and carried Bugna back to her stone house.

"This can't possibly happen now," Makanas said. "We need you to be strong to help us."

He gently placed the shaman on her couch. She looked too fragile and old.

Putot dashed through the door, followed by Mimi, ducking to avoid hitting his head. "Another one?" She rummaged through a cabinet. "Where is it? I'm sure Lin-ay put it back here somewhere."

"What anting-anting are you looking for? I can help." Makanas gripped his blade, and the house blinked with all sorts of anting-antings.

"The ylang-ylang." Putot closed a drawer, scattering herbs on the floor.

Lin-ay had said she sensed calm. Makanas tried his best to ignore other powerful anting-antings and sought calm. But the shaman had too many anting-antings in the house. It was like a sea of noise, and picking one from the others was impossible.

"I'll be fine," Bugna said from the couch, her voice

so weak that Makanas almost didn't hear her. "I'll probably just need to rest for a day."

Then Makanas felt a familiar power. *Lin-ay's anting-anting.* "Here!" he shouted in triumph. He pulled open a drawer and clutched the flower. "Why did you scream? What did you see?" Makanas asked as he placed the ylang-ylang into the shaman's palm.

"Lin-ay is locked in a room of dark magic. Also, Dungog knew you would come." Bugna avoided Makanas's eyes, and while Makanas didn't doubt she'd indeed seen what she just said, he knew she was hiding something else.

"Does looking at the future always weaken you?" he asked. "And why did you do it in the middle of the conversation? You could've picked a good time."

"Young man, I would've if I could." The shaman seemed to have recovered some of her strength, since she was even feigning irritation. "I wonder why Bulan listened to your prayer. Thanks to you, Lin-ay regained control of her body."

"Oh! Then I can do—"

"Hush!" Bugna pressed a finger to her lips. "From now on, you need to be very careful what comes out of your mouth. Dungog can see the future, like me."

"But I thought this forest was safe. He can't possibly hear us from here."

"He can. At least, before Bakunawa rises, when my power is at the weakest."

"What did you see? Why did you scream?"

Bugna sighed. "I hate to talk about this, but it might be better if you know." The shaman sat straight, her frail body turning youthful and strong. Her eyes were steely when she met his. "I saw you beheading your father."

Makanas shook his head. "Maybe you've lost your touch. Perhaps it was an illusion."

He'd imagined striking his father countless times, just to see how he would react to the pain, but that was only when they dueled. No matter how harsh Kidlat was with his training or how coldly he treated Makanas, he could never kill his own father.

"Be careful," Bugna said. "They might use tricks on you to distort your reality. You must be strong. Now, go and get yourself captured."

Bugna's vision of the future might have been limited, and she couldn't choose what she saw, but she was right about one thing—Makanas was going to get captured. Despite the bakunawa's power, he couldn't defeat Dungog and Datu Habagat's warriors. And she was right about something else, too. He needed to be careful about feeding magical blades with human blood. The blade's hunger to taste more and more blood didn't allow him to stop cutting.

Armed with anting-antings and years of fighting, Makanas had killed about a hundred men. His healing power had taken care of every cut, but no anting-anting would be fast enough to heal the wounds from the hundreds of arrows presently aimed at him. He sheathed his blade, smothering the hunger whispering at him.

Dungog raised a hand, and the arrows pointed at him were lowered. One warrior wearing pangayaw clothes blindfolded him, and another tied his wrists and dragged him. When the blindfold was removed, he was somewhere underground. His anting-antings were muted. Even the bakunawa blade tied to his waist felt like just a useless piece of metal. Leaving it there seemed like a mockery, for they knew he couldn't awaken it in the room coated with dark magic. He looked around and found Lin-ay sitting cross-legged, her back straight and her face serene.

"Just as you had predicted." Datu Habagat stood against the wall. He seemed to have come out of nowhere. He produced a thin knife and held it against Makanas's throat. "You ruined my reunification plan."

Makanas moved his head back as the knife sank into his flesh.

"Enough!" Dungog shouted. "You can't kill him now."

"You told me I'd have my revenge. I've let him go too many times already. Perhaps if I send his head back to Kidlat, that'll distract him for good." Datu Habagat's teeth were bared, his hand shaking.

Makanas wondered who was following whose orders. *Is Datu Dungog more powerful than Datu Habagat because of his visions? And why does Datu Habagat hate me so much?*

"Patience," Dungog said, emotionless.

Datu Habagat's blade moved from Makanas's throat to his face. "Fine," Datu Habagat said, emotion draining from both his voice and his face, a crack in his facade quickly covered. "I can't kill him now. Let me at least leave a mark on his face just like Kidlat did to my son."

Dungog shrugged.

Datu Habagat must have thought that was an agreement. "For Si Langit."

Hot, piercing pain shocked Makanas's whole body. But more than the pain, Datu Habagat's words made Makanas's head spin. *Si Langit. Si Langit.* The words played in his mind again and again like echoes, and the voice was sometimes a man's and sometimes a woman's.

"It's disgusting to see a warrior cry from such a small wound." Datu Habagat's voice seemed far away.

Lin-ay's screams sounded muffled.

The room was too hot. Fire was everywhere. Makanas looked up and saw Kidlat. Instead of helping Makanas, he slashed his face. Makanas screamed. His mother screamed a forgotten name. When he turned, he saw his mother's face, and everything became clear.

"Father." Tears streamed down Makanas's face as the flood of memories continued to pour. He understood why Kidlat had always been so cold and cruel to him. Every time he looked at Makanas, he must have been crushed from the inside. "Father, it's me, Si Langit."

"Don't you dare say that name with your foul mouth," Datu Habagat hissed.

And perhaps I shouldn't have, Makanas thought. *What use would it be for the datu to know that his son and the son of who he thought was his son's murderer were one and the same?* Mothers often spoke about how they would recognize their own blood, no matter how long they were separated, but Makanas, with all his anting-antings, had never once suspected that the man who'd raised him wasn't his own blood. All his hardship, all his sacrifices to gain Kidlat's approval now seemed pointless. Iyay had done a good job of playing a real grandmother, smothering any doubts he might have had since he was young.

He had no desire to play a son of an evil man, because attachment would only make it harder to kill Datu Habagat. No matter how wicked they might be, it was the nature of humans to respect their elders.

Datu Habagat's eyes widened, just as they had when Makanas was six, when blood flowed down Makanas's face. Raw anger followed, just as it had a long time before, when he had dashed to save Makanas, only to find his sword penetrating Makanas's mother.

Datu Habagat whirled, his hands circling Dungog's throat. "Did you know?" he roared. "Did you know?"

Dungog disappeared. When Makanas blinked, Dungog was standing against the wall, far from Datu Habagat's reach. "You must have misunderstood my power, Datu Habagat. I can glimpse the future but not the past."

"But you died." Datu Habagat knelt in front of Makanas. "I saw your head in a... box."

Makanas looked away. He didn't want his view of the man clouded. Datu Habagat was cruel. He couldn't justify his killings. He couldn't possibly have inflicted all those atrocities because of his son's death. Instead, Makanas focused on Lin-ay. The girl was as surprised as he was, perhaps wondering if Makanas had been acting.

"You can see the future. You would've known I was going to kill him." Datu Habagat stood and slowly approached Dungog.

Dungog stared unblinking, his eyes darkening. "Why, look at that. The future just changed." He swayed, as if he'd just lost all his strength. "This boy is going to behead Kidlat, not you."

"You knew." Datu Habagat's fist found its mark.

Dungog's face contorted with anger. He lifted a hand. He stormed out as the door opened. Datu Habagat glanced at Makanas before leaving.

Lin-ay knelt in front of Makanas and examined his face. "The bleeding has stopped."

He resisted the urge to touch his face. It didn't feel as painful as his other cuts. The memory only made it seem worse, but he ached everywhere. Without his healing anting-anting, every small cut on his body seemed to sing with pain.

"What are you going to do now?" Lin-ay asked, her eyes mirroring his conflicted emotions.

"I don't know. I wish I hadn't remembered." Then

he could've fought as the valiant warrior protecting his father's barangay.

"Dungog said you're going to kill your father." She lifted a cup of water. "It's fine. I drank from this. Dungog wants me alive," she said when Makanas shook his head. "You must not kill Kidlat. Even if you take control of the barangay, you'll lose the warriors' trust. Una, Dasig, and most of the people came because of the head warrior. But... I don't know what we're going to do to your real father afterward."

"I don't know." Makanas leaned back against the cold wall. He wanted to sleep and forget everything, just for a few hours. Talking about it didn't help. He winced as Lin-ay's cold hands touched his face.

"Be still. I'm going to clean the wound. I wish we had clean cloth here."

Makanas did his best not to wince as she gently poured water on his wound and slowly wiped the blood around it. Exhaustion pulled his mind away from reality, and he was glad. The past days had been nonstop preparation for Bakunawa's return and constant conflict between him and Kidlat. He thought he felt Lin-ay's soft lips before he slept.

He woke to bright light when the door opened. His first instinct was to grab whoever entered, but the door closed before he could stand. Fresh clothes, warm food, and boiled guava leaves had been placed on the floor. Water from the guava leaves could help his wound heal more quickly. Since Dungog had the decency to send salve for his wounds, Makanas thought Datu

Habagat must have convinced Dungog to keep him alive.

The next time they came to deliver food, he tripped a warrior and disarmed him, but twenty more surrounded him. He didn't expect to escape that easily. Even if he killed all of them, more would surely come. Without his anting-antings' power, he felt useless. His slowly healing wounds irritated him more. He and Lin-ay had no awareness of time, but based on the frequency of the food delivery, she suggested they must have been there at least two days.

"I'm afraid we'll be trapped here when Bakunawa rises," Makanas said.

Lin-ay nodded. "All we can do is wait."

So he slept, grateful that his dreams were no longer hunted by his mother's screams. Awareness of his anting-antings startled him awake. His hand automatically grabbed the hilt of his bakunawa blade, and he jumped to his feet, ready to defend Lin-ay.

Datu Habagat was standing at the door and looked from side to side. "Hurry. Before Dungog wakes up."

Makanas tilted his head in disbelief. He certainly didn't want the man's help, but he also wanted to free Lin-ay. "Why?"

"We will attack today. Dungog will exhaust your strength for days so that Kidlat will be weak when Bakunawa rises. You must take advantage of this opportunity when Dungog is resting."

"No." Lin-ay shook her head furiously. "Dungog has a tracker. He'll kill my mother when I escape."

"My spell will break in about an hour. You have to free the shaman on your own. I can't risk being seen by Dungog's warriors."

"Where?" Lin-ay's voice cracked. "Where's the shaman?"

"In the tree house, your father's tree house. You have to be careful. Dungog has warriors guarding it."

Makanas grabbed Lin-ay's hand as she dashed toward the door. "Follow me. You have to act as a bait just like we did with the demons." He turned toward Datu Habagat. "Don't expect me to spare your life when we meet again just because you helped us today." He didn't wait for the datu's reply.

Warriors were lying unconscious on the ground outside the underground door. As they raced through the yard, filled with sleeping warriors, he wondered just how powerful the datu was. Lin-ay pointed at the ruins of their house as she alighted. "Lin-ay. Let your spirit go."

"It's me. I didn't call the goddess."

Makanas skidded to a stop. "When did you get the anting-anting?" He gasped as an arrow hit her leg. "Duck!" he shouted as another arrow flew in her direction.

Lin-ay gritted her teeth and yanked the arrow out. Tears ran down her cheeks. He knew her anting-anting didn't take away the pain, but she faced it bravely, knowing she'd heal in no time.

"We have to fly fast." She pointed at the top of the hill. "Fast enough to not get hit."

"Are you okay?"

"Yes."

Arrows were flying from all directions as they neared the mountain, so they shot into the sky, high enough to escape them.

"We have one hour," Makanas said. "We can't keep on avoiding them."

"We don't have to." Lin-ay took something from her pocket. "I can't believe I forgot about this."

Makanas flew closer. "I don't see anything."

"This." She held her hand higher.

Despite the light from the moon, Makanas couldn't see anything. He shook his head in frustration, thinking they shouldn't be wasting their time talking.

"The hidden tree gave it to me. I'll go invisible and get the shaman."

Makanas wanted to argue. Bugna had told him the tree wouldn't give its power to anyone due to its rarity. He blinked as Lin-ay disappeared right in front of him. "Lin-ay?"

"I'm here."

Makanas felt a light tap on his shoulder. "Be careful. We don't know if some of them can detect anting-antings like my father."

9

THE CHANTER

Invisible, Lin-ay flew among the warriors without disturbing a hair on their heads. She finally reached the tree house without being detected, but opening the door would surely attract attention. She perched on a nearby tree and shook it just enough to get the guard's attention before landing on the stairs of the tree house.

"I'm here to free you," she whispered as she opened the door.

The boy inside was lying straight on the bamboo floor, a flimsy blanket covering his thin frame. He was the same shaman who'd tried to put a tracker on her in the underground room. Lin-ay knew better than to assume he was a child. He could have been thousands of years old, just like Putot.

"Don't be afraid. I'm not going to hurt you. I'll carry you out of here." Lin-ay knelt down to carry the boy. She jerked back as the boy sat up straight, black eyes staring right through her.

"I know you," the boy said. "But I'm no prisoner."

Lin-ay gasped as the boy transformed into a snake. It coiled around Lin-ay, squeezing the air out of her.

"I can sense you." The snake hissed.

Lin-ay wanted to speak, but the snake's grip was too tight. She'd never thought someone would work for Dungog willingly. She released her hold on her flying anting-anting, willing her body to break free, but the snake gripped her even more tightly. She had nothing else but a healing anting-anting that repaired her broken bones, but they were only crushed again.

"*Bulan*," she called.

The goddess didn't come, but Makanas did. Lin-ay's jaw dropped as her gaze focused on the bakunawa blade. Makanas had awakened the blade. He charged the snake, brought his glowing sword down, and severed the serpent's head. It grew back in an instant. Makanas turned for a moment as the warriors hacked at the door.

Lin-ay had no weapon. She needed something, anything sharp. Even as she peeled a bamboo strip from the floor, she knew it was ridiculous, but even that was better than her bare hands. She flew toward the snake's head, intending to poke the snake's eyes. It didn't matter if she failed. The snake just needed to focus on her for a moment.

The snake dodged.

"Its eyes!" Lin-ay shouted.

Then the door crashed, and the warriors tumbled in. *We're doomed.* Makanas turned and stabbed the snake right through the eyes. Then a lanky man posing as one of the warriors stabbed Dungog's warriors.

"Tanda!" Lin-ay gasped.

The lanky man hacked at the warriors, not letting even one past the door. He won't be able to hold them for long. The warriors had started hacking at the bamboo walls. The tree house would soon crumble from arrows and blades flying from all directions.

The snake writhed, but its bleeding had stopped.

"My healing anting-anting." Lin-ay had never suppressed it before like her invisibility power. She had to learn quickly before the snake healed completely.

Lin-ay concentrated on the ylang-ylang flower in her pocket. She sought the healing power, gathering every bit of it around her, and trapped it inside her own body. As the concentrated power gathered within her, she felt stronger, as if nothing could break her.

Makanas raised his blade, ready to bring it down the unmoving snake.

"Stop!" Lin-ay screamed. "You can't kill him."

Makanas turned, eyes wild, and Lin-ay could almost picture herself holding the powerful blade. The snake turned into a boy again, eyes still bleeding.

"Hurry! Dungog will wake up soon," Tanda said. He tossed a bottle to Makanas. "Feed it to the shaman. Keep him asleep and tie his hands with your father's spider's web."

Lin-ay grabbed the boy as the tree house finally collapsed to the ground. She flew and carried the boy as Makanas and Tanda deflected the arrows. They headed south. The boy was limp in her arms, but she didn't trust him to stay unconscious for a long time. "Let me do it." She held out a hand. Then she realized she was still invisible.

"Are you... the binukot?" Tanda asked. "How did you get such a powerful anting-anting?"

Lin-ay released her hold on her invisibility anting-anting. She bowed quickly to greet Tanda and grabbed the bottle from Makanas. She positioned the boy's head against her shoulders and opened his mouth. Then she slowly poured the liquid in.

"I have to go back," Tanda said.

"The warriors know you," Makanas said, gripping Tanda's arm.

"Those who saw me won't remember my face. I have to keep an eye on Dungog. Hurry before Dungog kills Amihan. He must have realized by now that you two have escaped. It won't be long until he checks the tree house."

"You've helped us twice now," Makanas said. "What can we do to return the favor?"

"It's no favor. I'm doing this to have a better future... and to make sure you slay Bakunawa."

"So you can see the future too!" Lin-ay blurted.

"Yes. But the future could change at any moment." He motioned with a hand to dismiss the topic. "You must fly as fast as you can. Wait," he added, as though remembering something. "Habagat might not want to kill you anymore, but he's bent on getting Bakunawa's power on his own. I think you need to know that, in case you're confident he's not going to harm you anymore."

"Can you tell me," Lin-ay asked, "if Makanas will kill the head warrior?"

"That hasn't changed… yet. Promise me we'll see each other again." Tanda disappeared into the dark night.

Lin-ay and Makanas flew quickly without speaking. Sulod's spell was so completely broken that they flew over the tree tunnel without getting snared by any illusions. By the time they reached the Bolo Warrior Barangay, the fog had cleared, giving them a perfect view of the rice terraces, like a stairway to the sky. Everything seemed perfect and calm until Adlaw's scream echoed through the mountains.

"Mother!" Lin-ay shot up to the plateau, Adlaw's scream guiding her.

Amihan's ashen face was nonresponsive when Lin-ay entered the meeting hall. She dropped the shaman onto the mat beside her mother. "Wake up! Wake up!" She shook the boy's shoulders, but he didn't move. "Wake up, you demon, and heal my mother!" she screamed.

"It's too late," Iyay said. "I could do a returning ceremony right now, but that'd only prolong her agony."

"He can heal her. He can remove the tracker!" Lin-ay screamed.

Kidlat dropped to his knees, opened the boy's

mouth, and smelled the boy's breath. "Sleeping potion?"

"Yes. Please hurry!" Lin-ay couldn't do anything but clasp her hands tightly.

"Everyone! Release your hold on your healing anting-antings." Iyay commanded as she rummaged through her bottles and herbs.

Lin-ay hadn't realized she was still holding hers in.

"Honey! Where's the magical honey?" Iyay circled around the room as women lifted bottles, checking each label and putting them back down.

"Here!" Kayay shouted.

"Thank you, dear," Iyay said as she poured it into another bottle. "But why are you here? You should be in the shelter."

Kayay backed away slowly, bowing her head. Kidlat held the boy's mouth open as Iyay poured in her concoction.

Lin-ay jerked backward when those completely dark eyes opened. *Unsettling.* She whirled and found Makanas standing still a few feet away. "Let me borrow your sword."

Makanas unsheathed his blade without question and handed it over. With a firm grip, Lin-ay rested the bakunawa blade on the boy's shoulder. "Remove your tracker. You are in the Bolo Warriors' territory. I'll kill you if you don't do as I say."

"Fine. I'll remove the tracker. But do you think you're in the right camp? Dungog has a greater chance. That's why I sided with him. You have the goddess in you. You are a goddess. You don't need anyone's help. You could swallow Bakunawa on your own. That's what gods do to increase their power. You're no diff—"

"Shut up and remove the tracker. Now!"

The shaman turned into a snake, and Lin-ay held her breath as its fangs sank into her mother's flesh. Then the snake slowly turned into a boy again. Kidlat tied his hands together with what looked like a spider's web, but thicker, and blindfolded him. He then took the boy down the stairs to the underground.

"Why isn't she breathing?" Lin-ay asked.

"Now we do the returning ceremony." Iyay straightened Amihan's body and put something black like charcoal on Amihan's belly, head, and both hands. "I need everyone to stay away." Iyay's hands moved quickly, and in no time, smoke swirled from the cauldrons next to Amihan's head and feet. "And I better not hear anything."

Lin-ay grabbed Adlaw's hand and whispered in his ear. "Mother's going to be okay, but you have to promise not to make a sound, no matter what you see." Adlaw covered his own mouth with his hand and nodded furiously. Lin-ay wiped the tears from the boy's eyes.

"Oh, great ancestors, guardians of the dead and the living, please hear this simple request from your descendants," Iyay began her chant as she circled Amihan. She turned toward Lin-ay and Adlaw and begged the spirits to have mercy on them.

Lin-ay clutched Adlaw's hand more tightly and prayed.

"Guide Amihan back to this earthly body." Iyay stepped over Amihan's body and continued circling as she chanted.

By the time Iyay stepped over Amihan's body the second time, Lin-ay could swear Amihan's eyelashes fluttered. She stepped to see closer, but Adlaw pulled her back. He scowled when she looked down at him, perhaps disappointed at her for not behaving while the ceremony was still ongoing.

Sorry, Lin-ay mouthed. She focused on Amihan again. When Iyay stepped over Amihan the third time, she thought Amihan's finger twitched. She looked around, wanting to see confirmation on other people's faces, but she found no surprised expression like hers.

If the returning ceremony was the same as her favorite children's story, Amihan's toes would move next. Just so, Amihan's toes moved ever so slightly, almost like a trick of the eye. Hope grew within Lin-ay's chest as color returned to Amihan's cheeks. Next, Amihan's stomach rose and fell with every breath. Finally, her eyes opened by the seventh step.

Lin-ay dashed after Adlaw as Amihan sat up. Amihan hugged them both, her brows creased with worry.

"What about Itay? Please ask him to return too." Adlaw looked up at Iyay, eyes bright with hope.

"He's happy now with your ancestors in the afterlife."

"He couldn't be happier than when he's here. I'm here."

Lin-ay rubbed Adlaw's back. "It's too late. There's no body to return to."

"Remember this, young man," Iyay said as she poured water over the cauldron of coals. "If you ever become as powerful as your father, you must learn as early as you can. To do a returning ceremony, the body has to be warm. The thread of life must not be completely severed, and the soul must not have crossed the cave to the underworld."

"There's no heaven?" Adlaw asked.

Heaven, Lin-ay thought. The foreigner pangayaws' concept of the afterlife seemed to Lin-ay like the pantheon. But tumandoks, her people, believed only gods and demigods resided there. The people were under Dilim's rule in the afterlife.

"I have no idea where that would be," Iyay answered. "Perhaps if a pangayaw is kind enough to point out where that is, I would know. But know that when your father is strong enough in the underworld, he could come here and guide you to become a strong warrior like him."

Adlaw gently removed Amihan's arm from around him. He stood straight, faced Iyay, and bowed down to his waist. "Thank you, Iyay for bringing back my mother."

Iyay ruffled his hair. "Now hurry and get back to the shelter. War is coming. Your role is very important. You must keep your mother safe."

Lin-ay carried her mother and Adlaw as she flew down into the underground again, followed by Makanas. She was afraid that if she took her eyes off them, Amihan's return would become just a dream. Slowly, she glided along the spiral stairs until she reached the bottom of the mountain.

"This is a lot to climb for you," she said as she repositioned Adlaw on her back. Thanks to Makanas's tip, she held only her mother's hand instead of carrying her on her back too.

"Takes me the whole morning to climb. Kayay is much faster," Adlaw said. "There!" He pointed at a door straight ahead. "That one has—"

"Hush!" Makanas said from behind. "Dungog might hear you."

"Who? Elder Dungog?" Adlaw asked.

"Yes. He's a bad man. He can see the future. Maybe he saw what you're going to say today if I don't stop you."

"I wish I could see the past." Adlaw sighed.

"Me too, Adlaw. Me too," Lin-ay said.

After several twists and turns, they finally entered a crowded room. She thought they might be in one of the mountains in the south of the Bolo Warrior Barangay, but she'd lost her sense of direction after a few turns. Just as in the warriors' stations, bright orbs decorated the walls and ceiling. Despite the fact that they were underground, Lin-ay didn't feel suffocated. She wondered if Dungog already knew the location, and when she looked at Makanas, he had the same worried look.

"Mother, I have to talk to the head warrior."

Amihan pulled her hand. "Wait. This… is just an assumption. I think you're strong enough to unite with your spirit.

Lin-ay shook her head. "I'm not ready."

"May the spirits and our ancestors guide you." Amihan hugged her tightly.

Lin-ay's tears threatened to fall. She broke free before the rest of the women shed tears together with them. She hugged Adlaw quickly and turned away.

"You promised!" Adlaw's voice echoed through the tunnels. "You have to win, and then you'll rescue my friends."

"I will!" Lin-ay shouted back, wiping the tears she'd finally allowed to fall.

10

THE BOLO WARRIOR

Makanas raised a hand for a halt as he heard whispered voices just before he and Lin-ay glided around a corner. With Bakunawa's rising just a week away, he couldn't put aside his suspicion that someone might be spying on them. He let go his hold on his hearing anting-anting and immediately picked up Una's voice.

"I have no regrets. Whether I die or survive this, I'm glad I was able to get my revenge."

Lin-ay poked her head around the corner then looked back at Makanas, wide-eyed. "Dasig and Una are kissing," she whispered.

Makanas pulled her aside. "Let's go up the other way."

"I can't believe Una likes Dasig. She's so strong and talkative and condescending," Lin-ay said when they were too far away to be heard, still shaking her head.

"I'm not saying Dasig isn't strong, but I think Una will always get her way if they ever get married."

"No. Dasig beat her in our training when we were younger. He came first. I was second." That loss had always been a humiliation to him, but it didn't seem to matter at the moment. "That was in Baskog's class. He couldn't beat me after we moved up to my father's training. The only difference is that there's no award ceremony and there's no end with my father's class."

"That's surprising. He comes off as someone who always follows orders."

"That's because he was instructed to follow my orders. Because I was supposed to be the future head warrior. Wait." Makanas tried to sense the anting-anting around him. Since awakening the blade, he'd learned how to sense them, but he couldn't distinguish one from the other yet. He figured he needed weeks to master that skill. "I think the head warrior's here in Head Guard Uwak's station." He turned his head up to the next floor above them and sped faster.

"You need to tell your father you've awakened the blade."

"There's no need," Kidlat said, suddenly appearing at the open door. "Have you forgotten that I could sense power?"

Lin-ay bowed and kept her head down. Makanas couldn't read her expression, but he suspected she was angry that Kidlat had imprisoned her just to keep her from going to Dungog's barangay. Perhaps she felt guilty, too, for escaping and wreaking panic in the barangay and getting warriors sent to look for her.

"Some things are better left unsaid. For now, let's focus on Bakunawa's return."

"Yes, Head Warrior!" Lin-ay replied.

"Understand?" Kidlat stared at Makanas.

"Yes, Head Warrior," Makanas said. As much as he wanted to, he couldn't erase the facts that Kidlat had tried to kill him when he was young, and that he wasn't truly his father. He mentally shook his head to focus on the problem at hand. "I think Dungog knew about the shelter." When Kidlat raised an eyebrow, Makanas explained that Dungog could see the future. He also detailed how Bugna had no control over what she could see, and that seemed true with Dungog's ability too.

"Both of you better get some rest." The creases on the head warrior's forehead deepened.

"We can't leave the shelter unprotected," Lin-ay argued. "And Datu Habagat said they were going to attack today."

"We have warriors surrounding the mountain," Kidlat said. "Their air warriors won't attack without their foot soldiers."

"They're not enough. Perhaps I could stay with them."

"No! You must stay beside me. You must stay in the head guard's station."

"I won't be fighting? I want to help."

"The moment you step out, Dungog and Habagat will get you."

"But—"

"Bugna told me Dungog might have seen the shelter," Kidlat said, "so it'll be guarded from above by Una and Dasig, using Bugna's weapons."

"The ones we used to kill the demons from the underworld? But she said it's dangerous to feed it with human blood."

"She decided the consequence weighs less than barangay people's lives."

"Where's the snare ball?" Lin-ay asked. "The one I should use to trap Bakunawa's soul?"

Kidlat's face turned crimson. "In the head guard's station. No. You shouldn't touch it now. I'll hand it to you when it's time. Get some sleep."

Makanas had just closed his eyes when bird calls echoed throughout the chambers of the underground. He shot to his feet and rose to the sky. A few moments later, the north awoke with fires and explosions. *How did they arrive so fast?* Dungog's barangay should be a week away on foot. Datu Habagat and Dungog's men marched in.

Bird calls echoed through the mountains as orders were passed from the underground. The mountain to the south rumbled like thunder. Rocks and soil rolled down the river, creating a dam. Dungog's foot soldiers continued their march despite the river suddenly drying up. Makanas sensed Baskog approaching the dam. Then Baskog's anting-antings ignited as he punched it, and water roared down the riverbed, smothering the fires and killing the enemies in its path.

Makanas flew north. Marching enemies weren't his concern. He was out to slash flying enemies. He released an arrow aimed at the strongest pulse of power. The man fell like a bird with broken wings. Makanas opened his palm to catch the arrow when it found its way back.

Another rumble from the south told him a second dam was forming. The mountain flattened. Enemies shouted encouragement to climb the mountain. The cries were then also silenced by raging water. Makanas flew down, his arrow finding enemies climbing up from the valley of death and sending them to their merciful demise.

The enemies kept coming. The Bolo Warrior Barangay's defenses were working, but the enemies were like endlessly marching ants. As the eastern sky turned orange, he saw the devastation brought to the forest. Dead bodies were scattered everywhere. The Bolo Warrior Barangay had lost only a few men. Their defenses were still strong, but Makanas knew Dungog wouldn't show up until the last minute. Those initial forces were just distractions, which was why Kidlat had stayed underground.

By noon, five mountains had been collapsed with landslides used as traps. The warriors with low-level anting-antings were exhausted.

Una speaking. Enemies have broken through the south barrier, Una said via bird call.

Makanas held himself in place, fighting the urge to check on them.

A few moments later, Una's bird call echoed through the mountains again: *Cleared*.

Makanas looked up, surprised at sensing an immense power above him, but he found no one. He dodged as a skull-sized explosive dropped from the sky. A ball of fire exploded far beneath him, creating a hole in the mountainside.

"Healer!" A warrior cried below.

Makanas aimed his arrow up at the sky. "Arrow. Find your mark."

He released a breath as the arrow flew straight. The bow quivered as he waited for the arrow, but it didn't return. Makanas unsheathed his bakunawa blade. The blade glowed, giving him away to the enemy. Power surged within him. Trusting, but not blindly, he let the blade guide him. Lightning streaked against the clouds. The blade absorbed the power before it could strike his body.

Another bolt of lightning ignited, giving Makanas a glimpse of the man hiding among the clouds. Makanas's arrow was lodged in the enemy's chest. The man looked like Dungog, frail and lean, but he was younger, probably in his forties. Their eyes met, and Makanas realized the "lightning" was coming from the man's anting-anting.

The man raised his blade, which glowed like the

bakunawa blade, and slashed the air. Lightning erupted from the blade, and Makanas slashed it. He needed to get near. The man rose and disappeared. Makanas flew after him. His eyes might fail him, but not his sense of power. Before the man could release another bolt, Makanas flew quickly, closing the distance between them.

The bakunawa blade found its mark, and the man's sword shattered. As the enemy's eyes widened in surprise, Makanas finished him without blinking. The headless body dropped into the river, and Makanas's arrow flew back into his hands.

He dove down, concentrating on finding the strongest anting-anting. The fighting seemed endless. His blade and arrow hungered for more, which must have been why Bugna had warned them not to feed her magical weapons human blood.

By the fifth day, arrows from the underground—their last line of defense—were firing. The flying enemies weren't many, but the enemy's ground troops continued marching without end. No matter how many lives his arrow took, more came marching. He wondered where they got such a large number of warriors. He flew lower to help the Bolo foot soldiers as the arrows from the plateau took care of the flying enemies.

Makanas thought he'd seen some of the enemies

before. Despite their injuries, they marched on. Some of them were limping. He frowned as the enemies stepped on their fellow warriors. Makanas gripped the hilt of his blade as he watched a warrior missing a leg hopping. He blocked all anting-antings from his senses and focused on the man but could not sense any power.

He flew south, calling the guard who'd created one of the landslides using bird calls, but he heard no answer. He called for the second guard stationed in the second mountain—no answer from them either. He gasped as the number of enemy dead dwindled, hoping his suspicion was wrong. Then dread swallowed him as he watched a dead warrior stand up and rejoin the march.

Frantically, he put both hands to his mouth to report with a bird call, but a ball of light flew in his direction, making him dodge upward into a cloud of smoke. Another ball of light came from above. His whistle came out muffled as smoke assaulted his lungs. He had to find who was controlling the dead warriors. Using the glow of the bakunawa blade, he searched for an exit from the sea of smoke. He longed for clean air. He thought he was going to pass out. Desperate, he thought his only chance was diving toward the river.

A strong gust of wind cleared the surroundings. An eagle's piercing cry followed, and its blue-gray eyes stared at him. The eagle's head, crowned with brown feathers, tilted as if trying to see if Makanas was dead. *"Ride."* The command was in Makanas's head, like he was thinking about it.

"I'm okay," Makanas said.

"Ride," The eagle insisted.

Makanas shook his head and put his hands against his lips to whistle. He coughed instead. Smoke blanketed them again. The eagle flapped its wings, banishing the smoke. Makanas landed on the eagle's back. He took a deep breath and made his report. "Thank you, Agila."

The eagle dismissed his words of gratitude. Like him, the eagle seemed focused on finding the source of the smoke. The eagle soared up so high that Makanas struggled to breathe.

"There!"

Even as he said it, the eagle was already approaching Dungog. A look of surprise ghosted Dungog's face, but only for an instant before he fled. The eagle chased the old man but stopped as they reached Sulod.

"Hurry!" Makanas shouted.

"No." The eagle brought him back down, a few mountains away from the Bolo Warrior Barangay.

There, he heard echoes of commands from Head Guard Uwak and Kidlat for him not to go too far. The eagle banked sideways, letting Makanas fall from its back, and disappeared.

Say thank you to Agila, came an almost incomprehensible bird whistle. *Lin-ay speaking.*

Had there been no battle, Makanas would have smiled. He hadn't known the girl was practicing the barangay's secret language.

As Makanas headed to the plateau, he noticed that the enemy had broken formation except for the few warriors heading them. Makanas suspected those who were still fighting were real warriors and not the dead who had risen. Without Dungog, the undead seemed to have lost their focus. He put his fingers against his mouth and whistled to relay his observation. Blazing arrows rained down on the undead as Head Guard Uwak determined fire would consume the bodies and stop them from coming.

Makanas had to find Dungog... quickly. He called for Dasig and Baskog's help through a bird call. "I can't sense Dungog's power," he said as four other warriors joined the search team.

"We have to lure him," Baskog said.

"With what?" Makanas asked.

"With you."

So Makanas wandered off the edges of their defenses, hoping Dungog would take the bait. The sun had set, and the number of the undead was dwindling, but nobody had sighted Dungog. Makanas switched his focus to the undead, shooting them again and again until their limbs could no longer rejoin.

On the night of Bakunawa's rising, Makanas circled the plateau, making sure everything was as planned. Iyay and other women gathered at a large table facing east, ready with their flutes. Everything seemed perfect, but

Makanas couldn't help but feel that something would go horribly wrong. He kept facing the east sea, leaving the rest of the defenses to Head Guard Uwak, just as Kidlat had planned.

At first, the change was subtle. Makanas thought his eyes must have been playing tricks with him when the sea swelled. But even with its calm surface, he knew the sea was rising. Chaos followed as the entire world seemed to tremble. Trees fell. Mountains moved. Even rivers changed their courses. His first thought was that the shelter would collapse, but then he remembered it had been made by Bugna with magic. He hoped Bugna's spell would hold.

The earthquake stopped, but the sea continued to rise. The water parted, revealing an endless abyss. Kidlat and Lin-ay were beside him in an instant. Dasig, Una, Baskog, and all the flying warriors protected the three of them in a circle. They set out, flying above the parted sea. Lin-ay carried a cloth bag with a something round inside.

Silence descended upon the earth as though the chaos was just an illusion. Makanas held his breath as the serpent rose. Its eyes were blazing red, just as described in the chants, but that didn't make Makanas fear it. He couldn't believe the serene creature was out to swallow the moon. It moved gracefully, as if the air was water. It was enormous but not as big as the legends had portrayed. Even its head was smaller than a *nipa* hut. Some demons that had escaped the underworld were bigger. He knew he should turn and watch out for Dungog and Habagat, but he found himself mesmerized by the flying serpent.

Kidlat dove, creating a shadow on the serpent's scales. Lin-ay followed. Kidlat landed on Bakunawa's back. The serpent stayed still. But when Kidlat unsheathed his blade, the serpent unleashed its fury. The blade glowed as Bakunawa's eyes blazed red with anger. Kidlat's strikes missed as Bakunawa used its tail like a whip. The two battled ferociously. For some reason, Makanas could sense the creature wasn't trying to kill Kidlat. It simply lashed at him when Kidlat blocked its way upward.

Makanas wanted to help but held himself back. Kidlat had ordered him to watch out for Dungog and Habagat.

The chant and the calming melody from the flutes made their way to Bakunawa. As the chant grew louder, Bakunawa grew more distracted. It stopped moving for an instant and appeared to tilt its head. Ignoring Kidlat, Bakunawa then flew toward the plateau, toward Iyay and the chanters.

Makanas flew ahead to make sure Dungog couldn't get close. A spark from above made him look up. Before the lightning could hit Makanas, he met it with his bakunawa blade. It was stronger than that of the other lightning conjurer, whom he'd met a few days before, but his blade still deflected it back up.

Dungog descended with Datu Habagat beside him. Dungog's hand opened to summon another lightning, but then he gasped. The lightning crackled and disinte-

The Bolo Warrior

grated. He looked down at his stomach. A bloody sword had gone straight through his back. He turned his head, eyes wild with anger at the betrayal. Datu Habagat withdrew his sword and swung. Dungog's head fell first, followed by his body.

Makanas, as shocked as Dungog's warriors, stayed frozen in the air for an instant. Datu Habagat took advantage of their surprise and, in quick succession, slashed at the warriors behind him. Others joined him. Makanas supposed they were Datu Habagat's men. The datu moved ruthlessly. In a few heartbeats, only about twenty of his warriors remained. He shared a meaningful look with Makanas before quietly flying away.

Makanas couldn't believe it. Dungog was dead, and Datu Habagat was no longer an enemy—at least, not at that moment. He appeared to be uninterested in Bakunawa's power.

Then an explosion rocked the side of the plateau. Bakunawa had struck the mountain with its tail, smashing Kidlat against it. Kidlat fell, and the bakunawa blade flew out of his hand. Lin-ay dove to catch it. When she rose, she was no longer Lin-ay.

She glowed as brightly as the blade. Bakunawa faced her, and just like a human would, dipped its head in a bow. The two faced each other, the chanting and the flute making their appearance even more serene.

"Lin-ay!" Makanas shouted. "I know you're in there. Lin-ay! It's me, Makanas."

Lin-ay stared back without recognition. Even at that distance, Makanas could see her ageless eyes. Kidlat lay unmoving on the rice terraces. He couldn't slay Bakunawa anymore. Lin-ay would have to do it.

"Lin-ay. Remember. Save the moon," Bakanas called out.

Lin-ay showed no reaction. Makanas flew toward her in order to get her to control Bulan. But even when Makanas reached her, he couldn't seem to break the moment Bakunawa and Bulan were sharing. They were just staring at each other in silence, yet Makanas knew the two were together in some way he couldn't fathom.

"Lin-ay, please. This is our only chance. You must slay Bakunawa. Now." Makanas dove toward Kidlat and sighed as Kidlat opened his eyes and held the blade up to him. As soon as Makanas's hand touched Kidlat's blade, he shuddered. The power was incomparable. *Perhaps I could slay Bakunawa.*

"Wake Lin-ay up and hand her the sword," Kidlat commanded.

Makanas bowed and flew back up to Lin-ay. Assuming she couldn't hear him, he decided to just speak to Bulan directly. "Hear me, Bulan, guardian of the moon. I'm here to help you."

Bulan turned those ageless eyes toward him. To his surprise, Bakunawa faced him too. The serpent circled Makanas, creating a ring around him with its body.

"Lin-ay! Break free! Protect the moon!" he shouted.

The serpent didn't touch him, but dread filled him.

"Makanas! Drop the sword!" Lin-ay shouted.

Makanas dropped the blade, grateful that Lin-ay had finally taken control of her spirit. When he looked down, the blade was floating toward Lin-ay, and he felt as though someone was watching him. When he straightened, red eyes were staring back at him, but Makanas was no longer afraid. Somehow, Bakunawa's eyes opened a gateway to memories he'd never had. Eager to know more, Makanas held Bakunawa's gaze, drinking in every bit of truth it offered, but then those red eyes closed, and the head slowly dropped. Before his mind could process what just happened, his soul was yanked out of his body. He struggled to follow his body plummeting along Bakunawa, but the force pulling him up was so strong. The last thing Makanas saw was the bakunawa blades raised and Lin-ay screaming her battle cry before darkness swallowed him whole.

PART III

All Bulan could do was hold Bakunawa's hand as gods debated about their punishment.

"And what about Bakunawa?" asked Puno, the leader of the shamans.

For the very first time, shamans had gained entry to the gods' realm, in order to join the council meeting. Puno was two hundred years old, yet his body appeared to remain at age forty, which was proof that humans were near the gods' level of immortality. If humans continued to progress and make new kinds of magic, they would surely soon surpass the demigods. That possibility created fear among the gods and had sparked a war.

"He, too, must be stripped of his memory. If not, he will help Bulan regain her memories, just like what happened last time," Dilim suggested.

"Then we'll be at the gods' mercy. Oh, great Bathala!" Puno's head touched the floor. "We are nothing compared to the gods who envied your affection."

Bulan doubted that said affection still existed in the creator. He had expressed on a couple of occasions that they had strayed from what he'd originally intended. He wanted their obedience and blind devotion. He also said that, perhaps, gods' intermarriage with humans, which he had also started, might have corrupted humanity. For even the demigods' children possessed powers beyond what Bathala had intended to grant.

"Perhaps humans are creations I shouldn't have made. I shall erase them from the face of the earth to restore peace among the gods," Bathala proclaimed.

"Perhaps you could punish Bulan and Bakunawa instead," Puno continued, his words hurried. "They led the demigods. Without them, we wouldn't have dared to fight the gods." His mouth kept opening and closing, but no more words came out.

Though the shaman strained to speak, Bathala didn't intend to hear any more of his words.

Anger consumed Bulan's reason. *How dare this human betray us?* If Bulan and Bakunawa hadn't defended the humans, the earth would have already shattered under the gods' powers even if Bathala hadn't ordered it. Bulan wanted to strike the man. But she came to a realization that perhaps other humans shared his sentiment only in order to preserve their own lives. If she wanted to kill every human out of anger for their betrayal, then she was no different from her father.

"Bathala, I shall do as the gods demand, but please let the humans live," Bakunawa said.

Puno found his voice again. "Thank you, Bakunawa."

"Even if there is no guarantee that your humanity will reunite with your god's spirit?" Bathala asked.

"Yes, Bathala." Bakunawa answered.

"Even if you might not see Bulan again?"

Bakunawa shared a look with Bulan. They both knew they would always find each other, whether as humans or gods.

"Yes, Bathala," they both answered.

Bathala nodded. "Gods and humans present, hear my pronouncement. I will let humans live. However, since they dared challenge the gods, they must be punished. They will no longer have access to the powers of the demigods. They shall face their adversaries on their own, and I shall obliterate those strong powers to keep them in place. To ensure that the gods will not harm them, I will close the door to earth, except the lake of life. No god shall set foot on earth without my approval."

Silence filled the council. Bulan held her breath, waiting for her punishment.

"Bulan will be stripped of her memories. However, she has been a good daughter to me and exposed those who were after my power. Because of that, I will allow her to live among the humans. She has to wait for the strongest human, both in body and will, to reunite with her memories. Bakunawa, as half human, will also be stripped of his memories. To prevent the two from meeting, his spirit shall be the guard of the afterlife, opposite the living."

"Power without memories could create a catastrophe," Dilim said.

"I am not finished!" Bathala roared.

Dilim was slammed down upon the floor, maimed.

"I am well aware they could get their memories back merely by wielding power. The moon shall keep some of their powers safe until they are ready to get them back."

11

THE CHANTER

Makanas was safe, and Bakunawa was dead. Lin-ay struggled to keep her balance as the snare ball moved on its own, pulling her down after the dead Bakunawa. At the back of her mind, her spirit was screaming, demanding her attention, but Lin-ay had grown stronger. For whatever reason, Makanas's voice had drawn her spirit out, giving Lin-ay the opportunity to grab Bulan's power and bend the goddess to her will. A stream of power left Bakunawa's body and entered the snare ball, which shook with such intensity that Lin-ay nearly flew upside down trying to control it. Then the source of power split into two. Lin-ay gasped as she realized what was happening. The other source of power was Makanas's body. Makanas was floating, not seeming to move.

Her spirit screamed for her to stop, but Lin-ay didn't know how to stop the foreign magic. It was sucking at Bakunawa's life on its own. When the stream of power entering the snare ball finally stopped, Kidlat was beside Lin-ay.

Her spirit gripped her, trying to force Lin-ay to let her through. Lin-ay refused, adamant that this wasn't the time to get those memories back. Before Makanas called Bulan earlier, Lin-ay had almost recovered all her memories.

Then Makanas was falling. Just like Bakunawa, he fell like a leaf. Calling Bulan must have exhausted him. Lin-ay threw the snare ball and the blade to Kidlat without a thought. She needed to catch Makanas before he hit the ocean and died.

She caught him by an arm and carried him like a child, thinking he should heal in no time. Lin-ay pressed a palm against her blouse's pocket, making sure that her ylang-ylang anting-anting hadn't been lost in the battle. Makanas's bakunawa blade dropped as Makanas's hand went limp, and Kidlat dove after it.

Bakunawa's body hit the ocean and disappeared without a trace. The moon was still shining above. The snare ball disappeared into Kidlat's body, making him grow even more brightly.

They'd won. Bakunawa could not torment the future generations any longer. Kidlat had enough power to punish the pangayaws.

"Makanas. We won. You did a good job." Lin-ay touched his cheek.

He didn't move. Her healing anting-anting seemed to have no effect on him. With trembling hands, she checked his nose for a sign of breath—nothing.

She had to hurry. Iyay could do a returning ceremony. But as she rose, returning to the plateau, Kidlat glowed as bright as the sun. He homed in on her, bakunawa blade raised. Without a doubt, Lin-ay knew he was going to kill her.

But why?

She had no chance of survival. Bakunawa's power was in Kidlat's body.

She let her guard down and her spirit in. Instead of fighting Kidlat head on, Bulan fled. Lin-ay no longer felt the confidence she had when her spirit was in her body. Instead, despair and mourning filled her. Lin-ay didn't understand why she was afraid of Kidlat. She was a god. Then she remembered something. Right before Makanas called Bulan earlier, she remembered how the blades had been forged. They had been a part of her, her own power she willingly gave to humans before the gods ripped her humanity away. She hadn't recovered all her memories, but Lin-ay suspected Bulan could sense Kidlat was more powerful than she.

"Hurry!" Lin-ay told herself. She was aware of the spirit's own mind within her. She had to get to Sulod. Perhaps Bugna could do the returning ceremony. "Hide us somewhere. You're a god."

The swirl of emotions made Lin-ay dizzy, and memories flooded back. She shook her head, needing to concentrate.

Datu Habagat flew toward her with his warriors. Behind them were Bugna and Putot.

"We'll distract him," Datu Habagat said.

"Bulan!" Bugna shouted. "The future was shrouded. But now I see that I was wrong all along. You must reunite with Lin-ay."

Lin-ay wanted to ask Bugna how, but Bulan's sense of longing to see her mother won out, and she shared her spirit's mixed happiness and regret at reuniting with Bugna at a time of distress. Behind her, she could hear Kidlat's rage as he fought with Datu Habagat and his men.

"I must regain all my memories first. Without it, this human body could perish." The words weren't Lin-ay's but of the spirit with its own consciousness in her. For the first time, the spirit and her soul had the same goal. "But first, we must keep this boy alive."

"Go!" Putot shouted. "I'll help distract Kidlat."

"Stop this madness this instant!" Iyay shouted. Iyay couldn't fly, but Una held her hands and made her look like she was flying. She urged Una to fly forward into the battle raging between Kidlat and Datu Habagat.

Bugna held up a hand. Lin-ay screamed as Kidlat's blade went straight through Iyay's body, and her spirit was ejected like a foreign object. Lin-ay wanted to turn and heal Iyay, but in a blink, they were in a foreign land. In another blink, the surroundings had changed again. When they finally stopped traveling, they were facing a lake shimmering with gold, purple, and white. In the center was a gigantic tree with leaves fresh and green with life, a stark contrast to all the death they'd just left behind.

"Iyay! I can heal her," Lin-ay said. "Take care of Makanas. I'll be back as soon as Iyay's healed."

She could feel her spirit's desperation as it begged Lin-ay to be called back into her body.

"Iyay wouldn't want you to go back."

"But she's going to die!"

"And so is this boy. Now, call your spirit back. We need her to enter the lake of life. This is partly the gods' realm. This is where life began, the opposite of the afterlife, and the only place Bakunawa couldn't reach. Kidlat can't harm you here." When Lin-ay didn't move, Bugna turned dead serious. "I wish I was as powerful as a god. Then I would have all the answers for you. But I'm not, and I have helped Kidlat do something despicable. I have underestimated his greed. But even if I hadn't helped him, Dungog would have done worse. Iyay isn't dead. And she won't be for a while. Now, call your spirit back so we can extend this boy's life. You need him."

Lin-ay suspected Bugna was lying to stop her from going back. Shamans were known to bend truth. In the silence they shared, Lin-ay was able to think critically. If she went back to aid Iyay, a high chance existed that Kidlat would swallow her spirit to gain her power.

Come to me. Her fear of the spirit's grip on her body lessened even though Makanas wasn't conscious to distract the spirit when she needed him to. She felt stronger and hoped her confidence was enough to free herself from the spirit when the time called for it. This time, when the spirit entered her body, it was subtle.

Lin-ay didn't feel that whirlwind of emotions. She faced the lake of life. She was surprised at the anger she felt. *How could I feel anger at the sight of a place partly my home?* With the goddess in her, she could see purple light surrounding the lake, which emanated an unearthly power of protection. Slowly, she flew toward it. Her body vibrated at the resistance. She was afraid her body would break with the pressure, but the confidence in her spirit told her to move forward. She sighed as she finally broke through the barrier. Then she turned back and nodded to Bugna. The shaman flew beside her and held her arm.

Bugna groaned in pain and fell to her knees as soon as they got past the light protecting the lake. But she said, "I'm going to be fine. Place Makanas down." She patted the soft grass.

Lin-ay placed Makanas down gently. "It is time I get all my memories back," she found herself saying. "I trust you to strengthen his thread of life, Mother."

She flew over the shimmering water and dipped a toe in. Her whole body pulsed. Feeling more alive than ever before, she let her memories come in. Time meant nothing. She knew her mortal body wasn't ready, but she had to try. That was her best chance of saving Bakunawa.

Hot, piercing pain ignited in her belly as her mortal body's thread of life braided with her spirit. The agony went on and on as she struggled to keep the braid from coming undone. Her body collapsed, sinking into the lake of life. She had to continue. The thread of her life thinned before her eyes. It was about to snap. Her goddess's spirit was too strong, burning her mortal life.

A distortion in the water broke her concentration. In the distance, Lin-ay could see Bugna in a panic, trying without success to untangle the braid of two threads of life. Then thunder hit the water, sending Bugna flying back to the ground. Lin-ay's braid broke, and the spirit was ejected from Lin-ay's body in a sharp pull.

"Father!" Lin-ay shot to her feet.

She knew just before her spirit had separated from her that Bathala's power was what had hit the earth. Bathala didn't want her mortal body in the god's realm, and that what had saved Lin-ay. She had to merge with her spirit. If she succeeded in doing that, she could possibly ascend to the gods' realm and seek help. Awareness of her surroundings returned. She was standing knee-deep in the lake. The shimmering water didn't feel hot or wet. Rather, it filled her body with such energy that she felt she could run forever. Makanas, or rather Bakunawa, lay face up a few feet from her. Half of his body was submerged in water.

Bugna lay crumpled on the ground a few feet away from the lake, blood pooling around her. Bulan dashed toward the shaman and pulled her toward the lake. She watched in amazement as the shaman's body healed in just a blink.

"Fool!" Bugna said. "How many times have I told you your body wasn't ready? It needs lower-level anting-antings. Lower power first. Your body would've been a hollow shell. Bulan would've—"

"I am Bulan, Mother. From this moment, call me Bulan, whether I have the spirit in me or not. For me to be strong and ready for the reunification, I need to accept the truth that the spirit and I are one. Before the gods tore my spirit away, I was a demigod with one consciousness. Lin-ay is just a name in a lifetime of my many mortal lifetimes."

"Did you... recover all your memories?"

"Not all, but I remember crucial information." Bulan sat on the soft grass. "The bakunawa blades are a part of me. I gave them to the people to protect the moon from Makanas, or Bakunawa."

"Oh, Bathala! Have mercy on us!" Bugna cried, her head on the ground. "Bakunawa... Don't tell me..."

"Yes, he was also a demigod stripped of his spirit and memories, like me. He's not an evil god." Bulan sighed. "Now Kidlat is more powerful than I because he has some of my powers, as well as Bakunawa's. Oh, how foolish I was to think that I, Bulan, was the most powerful god." She chuckled.

Bulan and Bugna brainstormed how to defeat Kidlat. Each of their plans came to a dead end. They didn't have enough allies.

"Datu Habagat might have been merciless, but Makanas... I mean Bakunawa, is still his son," Bugna said.

"I'm not sure he's willing to lend me his anting-antings."

"He will. Bakunawa can't stay in the lake of life forever."

Bulan knew that too. Even the lake of life could not keep a mortal body alive for long without the soul.

"I will find Habagat for you. You must not leave until I return. You need Habagat's concealer to hide from Kidlat."

"I could get one from the afterlife myself."

Bulan realized as soon as she said it that the task was impossible for her to undertake. In the eastern sea was the cave called Yungib, a gate to the underworld that housed the evil humans imprisoned by Bathala during the human's revolution. They were beyond redemption and had lost their humanity. Reduced to animals, even their bodies had transformed. The ones they'd fought before were merely those nearest the mouth of Yungib. Even if she could possibly fight them, Dilim, the god of the underworld, could possibly wake and punish them for breaking in. However, Bulan knew she couldn't possibly avoid the journey to the underworld. To resurrect Bakunawa, they would have to put him back to Yungib, in between worlds, where his power was the strongest.

When Bugna left, Bulan crouched next to Bakunawa and wondered how she could have forgotten his face. He looked exactly the same thousands of years ago. Bulan breathed in and summoned her spirit. When the two consciousnesses were in her body, she saw things her human eyes couldn't. She saw Bakunawa's thread of life, vibrant, running from his belly button down into the water. He seemed to be drinking life from the lake.

She stepped into the water and headed deeper,

aware of her two threads of life braiding again though she wasn't trying to merge with her spirit. Bugna wasn't there to call her back if something went wrong. The water reached her chin, but she wasn't afraid. She breathed in as water covered her mouth. When she was finally completely submerged, she saw the roots of the tree in the center of the lake. They pulsed and released vibrant colors. She was very close. When she reached out to touch the tree, a violent wave tossed her back onto land.

Bulan sighed. "Well, Father, you're still as merciless as ever. Or perhaps you don't even know what mercy is." She watched the water drizzle back into the lake from her skin, as if the lake couldn't afford to lose even a drop. Bulan had hoped Bathala would grant her entry to the gods' realm. She had been trapped in an endless loop of rebirth for thousands of years and hoped that time had somehow erased some of her father's anger. She chuckled. Time had no meaning to the gods. She had indeed lived a long time as a human, for even when her spirit was in her, her thoughts and her behavior were more human than godly. She wondered if that would remain the same once she successfully merged her soul and spirit.

She looked around, wanting to find an anting-anting to slowly introduce to her body. Her spirit stirred at the thought. *Bakunawa.* She scrambled to her feet, deciding that wielding the blade would be the best way to strengthen her body. Disappointment settled in her heart as she looked at the empty scabbard tied to Bakunawa's waist. She remembered Kidlat had dove after it after Makanas fell unconscious. Since Kidlat had five blades, he was half as powerful as Bulan. Combined with Bakunawa's power, Bulan didn't stand a chance unless she rejoined with her mortal body.

Bulan eyed Bakunawa's headscarf. The tiger's hair woven into it outshone the rest of his anting-antings.

"I'll return it to you." She kissed his forehead and untied the cloth.

Then she tied the headscarf around her head and pushed her spirit away. Strength and agility coursed through her body. She ran around the lake of life, imagining an enemy and practicing the moves Una had taught her. She leaped as far as she could. She wished Una was there to help her. Even the young Kayay would have been helpful in strengthening her core. With constant use of anting-antings, a human's soul would become stronger, more suitable to higher power. Thousands of years before, anting-antings that slowed down aging were plentiful. That was how people had ascended into power that almost equaled the gods. The gods only realized the importance of time as more and more people defeated demigods.

Bulan waited, stretching her patience to the point of snapping. Bugna had said she would return in a day, but she didn't.

12

UNA

Carrying Iyay, Una flew as quickly as she could, trying to stay near Kidlat. Her own healing anting-anting was pathetically weak against Iyay's wound. Her eyes felt hot, but she would not cry. Tears were reserved for the dead, and Iyay couldn't die. Una would not allow it. The old woman had been the first to hold Una in her arms when other women and children avoided her. Iyay was the one who'd protected her when she was almost banished for failing to make anting-antings work.

The air itself seemed to boil with rage as Kidlat screamed. Lin-ay and Bugna had disappeared in a blink. Kidlat must have realized his mistake of wasting his time fighting Datu Habagat. He ignored the datu and flew away at the speed of lightning, without a doubt, to look for Lin-ay and Bugna.

"Don't you die on me, old shaman. You have to heal my wounds." Una desperately wanted to sound brave, but her voice cracked. Slick blood wet her arms as she hugged the old woman, feeling the liquid seep through her blouse.

Kidlat returned. Una would have pressed her head to the ground in gratitude if she weren't flying.

"Mother! Tell me where that traitor hid Bulan." Kidlat's words escaped through gritted teeth. He reminded Una of the wild demons they'd fought at Sulod, which had escaped from the afterlife.

"She's badly injured. I'm afraid she's going to die, Head Warrior." In the back of her mind, Una wanted to slap the head warrior for not healing Iyay immediately. She couldn't believe healing his mother wasn't his priority.

"I know you can hear me, Mother. I will release my healing anting-anting, but if you don't tell me where they are, I will send you to the afterlife, where you'll eventually meet your friends."

Una couldn't even gasp in shock. She stopped breathing, unable to say a word. She had always thought the head warrior was cruel, but only to Makanas. She finally released a breath when Iyay grunted, her first sign of life.

Kidlat flew up behind Una, facing Iyay. "Now, where could Bugna have hidden Lin-ay?"

"Sulod," Iyay said in a breathy voice.

"No. Even that place can't hide anting-antings from me."

"Then why would you expect me to know? You know more about anting-antings than me." Iyay coughed, unable to continue. After the bout of coughing ended, she swallowed and spoke again. "Save your son."

"He is not my son."

"He is your son. Anyag's son is my grandson."

The wind slapped them aside as Kidlat flew away in fury. The revelation shocked Una. She had never understood Kidlat's cruelty toward his son. If Makanas was Anyag's son, that meant Kidlat's wife had bedded another man. But Kidlat's respect to her soul during ceremonies for the dead made Una doubt Anyag had betrayed Kidlat. Una wondered why he'd raised Makanas. Anyag was long dead. Knowing the truth made her want to turn her back on Kidlat even more.

That wasn't the first time she'd doubted the head warrior. After Makanas returned from his first mission, Una had been convinced he could lead the barangay better than his father. She hated his cruelty. All those years of being a kind warrior seemed like just a mask, now peeled off. She wished she hadn't ignored what she'd seen back then. Perhaps she should've told Iyay about Makanas's unjust punishment, but she didn't know whether that would have made any difference. She could no longer trust Kidlat. He was no longer the head warrior she respected. She feared he would slaughter all his people in his anger. Needing to talk to Dasig, she headed back to the Bolo Warrior Barangay.

Makanas needed to be found. But she didn't know where were they going to find him or if he was even still alive. He'd fallen like a leaf when Bakunawa died.

Una's stomach was hollow with dread. She was sure Kidlat was going to kill Bulan, and Lin-ay would also die because Bulan was in her body. She finally understood Kidlat's obsession with killing Bakunawa. He'd been after power all along. Bulan's power would perhaps make him as powerful as the gods. Even if Makanas survived, Una was sure he would finally turn his back on the barangay when Kidlat killed the one he loved. She prayed Kidlat wouldn't find Lin-ay.

Iyay was silent, simply resting her head on Una's shoulder. Una was thankful that the short moment with Kidlat had healed Iyay's major wounds. Although she was still losing a lot of blood, Iyay was slowly healing from Una's anting-anting. She flew down the spiral stairs of the underground at a dizzying speed. People greeted her with wide eyes when she finally reached the refuge. She was apparently the first to return from the battlefield.

Una lay Iyay gently on a straw mat, careful not to open her fresh wound. A woman who'd been Iyay's assistant bolted into action and immediately poured a green liquid onto Iyay's wounds. Una ignored a barrage of questions, her eyes focused on Amihan and Adlaw.

"You must get Amihan out of here," Iyay said, grabbing Una's wrist. "Now. Before he returns."

"Where?" Una asked, fearing Kidlat would find them.

"Anywhere. He can't find them as long as they don't bring any anting-antings." Iyay coughed again.

"Why?" Amihan asked. "Where's Lin-ay?"

The Bolo Warrior

"She's safe, dear. Bugna's with her. She can't return here for a while, but I promise you she won't be in harm's way as long as you are not here. You must go right away. Do not trust anyone except Una."

"I'll go with her! I'll protect them," Liwayway said, taking Adlaw's hand.

The confused boy flicked his eyes between Una and Iyay.

"I can't carry the three of you," Una protested. "I can only hold two hands."

"I'll carry the boy," Liwayway said.

"Go now, Una! Bulan's survival depends on you," Iyay said.

Una held hands with Amihan and Liwayway and flew. Before she turned a corner, she heard Iyay warning the people not to speak about Amihan's disappearance. Una prayed that Kidlat was still looking for Lin-ay. If he found Una helping Amihan escape, he might put Una to death on the spot. The plateau was empty when she finally emerged from the underground. The warriors might have been busy looking for Lin-ay. Kidlat had ordered everyone to look for her. She hurried south because she feared Kidlat was in the north, possibly near Sulod, hoping to find Lin-ay there. She flew low, using trees as cover, not wanting her fellow warriors to see her.

The problem was where to put Amihan. She couldn't stay away from the barangay for a long time. She expected the people to give her away, but she wanted Amihan long gone before Kidlat could get to her. For a moment, she thought of staying with Amihan, but she couldn't turn her back on Dasig. Kidlat knew their relationship. If Una disappeared, Dasig would be the first one tortured.

"Tell me what's going on," Amihan said.

Una could tell the woman was trying not to sound impatient. "I'm thinking. I don't know where you can stay. Far from Kidlat."

Nothing but mountains were ahead of them, but far to the south was a desert, and beyond that, the sea. They wouldn't survive there even if Kidlat couldn't find them. And if others found them, she feared they might capture Amihan simply because she was a datu's wife.

Una thought about killing them, give them a quick death to spare them more pain while keeping Bulan and Lin-ay alive, but she knew she couldn't possibly murder innocent people. Exasperated, she released a loud breath. "Damn the spirits. It's hard thinking alone." So she told the others about what had happened. She also told them they might be made hostages in order to lure Lin-ay back to the barangay.

"Just leave us here in the mountains," Amihan said. "Lin-ay will need you. So will Makanas. You can't die for disobeying the head warrior."

"No way. Lin-ay will kill me."

"My sister is that strong?" Adlaw asked with wide eyes.

"Perhaps stronger than anyone alive, but she doesn't know that yet," Una said. "Liwayway, do you know a place you can hide?"

Liwayway shook her head. "But I can keep them alive here in the mountains."

Adlaw screamed as Bugna appeared out of thin air. "Lin-ay!"

Bugna introduced herself quickly. Even though the shaman had ageless eyes, her body was young, and her face looked exactly like Lin-ay's. Adlaw continued calling her his sister.

"Return to the barangay, Una," Bugna said. "I'll bring them somewhere safe. Kidlat can't track me."

"Where will you bring them?" Una asked.

"It's better for you not to know." Bugna raised a hand, and everyone else disappeared.

When Una returned to the plateau, Kidlat was speaking with the flying warriors. She approached her fellow warriors slowly, not wanting to attract attention. Kidlat gestured to summon the warriors forward as more of them landed on the plateau. Head high, Una ran and stood next to Dasig.

"All here!" Baskog announced.

"Thanks to you," Kidlat shouted, "our barangay is now the most powerful on earth. Our names will be known for generations. We will rule other barangays. Our lands will stretch throughout the earth. Those who've died today will be honored! Especially my son."

Una could feel the rigid shoulders of her fellow warriors, especially the younger ones who'd trained with Makanas. Kidlat didn't allow their feelings to bloom.

"You will be given people to serve you and till your

lands. Not everyone will submit to my rule. I still have a lot to do. And you, my strongest warriors, will continue to help me. I have the perfect solution for you. I have Bakunawa's power in my body. Bakunawa guarded the boundary to the underworld. Now that he's dead, souls will come pouring in."

Una was glad the women and children were still in the shelter. They would've have been crying in horror. Perhaps the barangay people would have blamed Kidlat for killing the serpent. She kept a calm expression despite her boiling rage. If she'd been her old self, she would have hurled words at Kidlat despite his rank.

"Those who submit to my rule and chant a prayer will be free from the souls. Those who refuse will wander the earth as ghosts and watch as other souls possess their bodies. It's your task to spread the word."

Una clenched her fists. The people had no choice. She wondered what would happen to her next. Even if she chanted, her devotion would fail because she already had doubts in her heart. She would kill herself before that happened. A warrior to her left dropped to the ground as blood sprayed the brown soil. A knife was in his hand, a few inches from his neck. Kidlat nodded, and another warrior dragged the dead man away.

"You can follow him to the afterlife if you don't like me," Kidlat said without emotion.

Una's mind raced. The sword on her waist suddenly felt heavy. She had no regrets. She'd gotten her revenge.

Her parents were at peace in the afterlife. Dasig took her hand before she could grab her hilt, and they shared a meaningful look. Una couldn't die now. They had to help Lin-ay. They had to die fighting. Una nodded in understanding, and Dasig slowly let go. Their shared moment was lost among a short chaos as more warriors killed themselves. An older warrior, about fifty, murmured a short prayer to his ancestors before slicing his neck with his sword. Una jerked back as his blood hit her in the face. The plateau was filled with bloodshed, not from any enemy's blow, but because of their own leader. Her vision dimmed, and she could barely control her rage.

"This is how you do the prayer." Kidlat put a hand to his belly. "Here is your thread of life. Protect it. Cover with your hand so no soul can enter your body. You must memorize the words."

Una breathed deeply. She needed to control herself. Dasig's hand brushed hers, giving her comfort. Just as Kidlat had trained them to be mentally strong, Una buried her hatred deep within, protecting it with layers and layers of other emotions. She had to convince herself first that Kidlat was good and that she was on his side. She thought of the good he'd done. She thought of the time when she was young and he rescued her. She thought of the skills he'd taught her. Finally, she made herself think that there could be no other person who could lead them but him. The world would be better with his leadership. He'd defeated Dungog and even Bakunawa. If he killed Bulan, he would be more powerful, and no one could subject them to harsh rule again—no more torture. Deaths would be quick. Kidlat's silence allowed the warriors to prepare themselves mentally. When he finally spoke, Una's heart was ready to listen. The calmness she felt was no longer a facade.

"Kidlat the Great..." Kidlat paused, waiting for the warriors to follow his words. "Guard of the underworld..." He paused again. "Protect me. In your rule, I am safe. My life is yours." He repeated the same prayer three times. "By now, your body should be safe. If you only pretended, your life is forfeit. Understand?"

"Yes, Head Warrior!" the warriors chorused.

"As I have promised, I will give you lands. Let's start by taking over Tago town. Mariit Inn will be my residence from now on. Bring me slaves to serve me. Start spreading the word to our people in the shelter first and then the town. We don't need to hide here in the mountains anymore. Order our people to move to town!" He took a big breath. "The fight isn't over. I will keep looking for Lin-ay. She is now my enemy. Do not try to fight her. You will die. Bulan, the half goddess, is using her body now. Report to me immediately when you find her."

13

THE CHANTER

Bulan jogged around the lake of life to keep herself from overthinking. Three days had passed since Bugna left. Bulan was growing more anxious. Though she never felt hungry when she was touching the water from the lake, she longed to eat. She never dared to step outside the lake of life to hunt for food. Even though she was a goddess, she didn't have the ability to teleport like Bugna could. She knew Bakunawa didn't have that power either. When her shadow finally disappeared beneath her feet and the sun was straight above her head, Bulan slowed to a halt when she saw Bugna approach the lake of life. She closed her eyes and invited her spirit back to her body. Doing so had become as easy as inhaling.

Bugna's face was unusually pale, for a shaman who didn't age. "Kidlat has become completely evil in his greed. Souls are pouring in from the afterlife, possessing the living. If this goes on, the souls of the living won't be able to find their way back. Bakunawa needs to wake up and seal the boundary to the afterlife." She grunted as they passed by the light protecting the tree of life. "Perhaps you could talk to the gods. Tell them the world is breaking apart."

"I need to be a demigod before I can ascend into the gods' realm. Human lives are nothing to the gods, especially now that they believe the era of magic is over and humans can never challenge them again. This is what Dilim wanted, but he couldn't do it himself, for fear of Bathala's wrath. With Kidlat's greed, he's helping Dilim take over the land of the living."

"Oh dear spirits." Bugna reached into her purse and held out a concealer. It looked like Kidlat's snare ball, used to trap Bakunawa's soul, but only half. "Habagat has the other half. It'll conceal your location from Kidlat, but it won't work if you're too close."

Bulan already knew that. She couldn't use surprise to attack and retrieve Bakunawa's spirit. "Has Habagat completely changed his mind?" she asked as her hands closed around the concealer.

"It's hard to say. The man had darkened his spirit with blood and hatred for a long time before he knew his son was alive. I know light still exists within him, pushing him to do good, and he's desperate to get his son back." Bugna's eyes hardened with resolve, a look that most mothers shared, throughout Bulan's many lives on earth.

"Any news about Amihan?" The name felt strange on her tongue, but calling Amihan *Mother* in front of Bugna, who was also her mother, would've felt stranger.

Bulan expelled her spirit. "Has anyone seen Mother?"

"She's safe. I brought her somewhere Kidlat couldn't find."

"You could have brought her and Adlaw here."

"You can't be in the same place. Even though Bakunawa's power doesn't work here, Kidlat still has many anting-antings. And did you forget he has the bakunawa blades? If he tracked you here, Amihan would also be in danger. I can guarantee their safety, so you must focus on preparing yourself fast."

Bulan wanted to know their location at least, but instead, she said, "I trust you."

"Kidlat has created a spell. Anyone who surrenders to his rule won't get possessed by the souls. The world has fallen into a new chaos. People are killing themselves."

"Why did he have to go to such great lengths?" Bulan knew the answer was greed because humans were created like gods, who lived to follow their greed, and humans were no different, seeking followers and adoration at the cost of lives. "I have to be powerful. Fast." She eyed Bugna's purse. "Habagat gave you something else too."

"Ah, yes. But I don't know if you're ready." Bugna

handed Bulan the purse. "Some of them are mine, from back when I was still hunting anting-antings. I have something else to tell you." She rolled her sleeves up to her shoulders, showing two fresh bite marks marring her porcelain skin.

"Have you gone mad? Why did you let Habagat put a tracker on you?" Bulan fumed. Seeing the tracker marks brought back memories of pain, of Bakunawa's cries, and Amihan's death.

"I'm strong enough to fight Habagat if he decided to use it to give me pain. This is the only way for me to communicate with him even if he's on the other side of the earth. I need to know what he's doing." Bugna unrolled her sleeves.

"You didn't have to go that far. Habagat has done horrible things. We can't trust him."

"I threatened to kill his son if he decided to do something funny."

Bulan turned toward Bakunawa, lying half submerged in the lake of life, and remembered how Datu Habagat had freed them from Dungog's underground. He'd risked his life back then. Then the scene of him killing Dungog in the end had convinced Bulan he did indeed love his son.

Bulan practiced with the anting-antings, starting with the lowest power level. The best way to get used to it was to use it for fighting, so she sparred with Bugna and was surprised that the shaman was not only good at using magic, but was also a strategic fighter. They fought ferociously, Bugna matching Bulan's skills.

"How come I can't sense your anting-antings?" Bulan asked after Bugna pinned her to the ground.

"Because they were fully absorbed by my body," Bugna said, raising an eyebrow. She got off Bulan and held out a hand to help her up.

Exhausted, Bulan put her hands on her knees. She'd been practicing with the anting-antings and fighting with Bugna for the whole day and had the urge to summon her spirit to see if her thread of life had improved, but she was afraid to be disappointed. Absorbing magic completely was new to her. Even those who rose to rebel against the gods thousands of years ago had failed to do it. Some had tried and died.

By several days later, Bulan had tried all the anting-antings, but none had really satisfied her. However, her constant rejoining with her spirit had strengthened her thread of life somehow, so she decided to try to reunite with it once more.

"You are not ready," Bugna protested.

"I know. But my thread of life has strengthened since I last tried."

"I can see that. But the risk is too high. I was barely able to distract you last time. I don't know if I can again."

"I'll stop as soon as I sense danger."

"Trying alone is danger enough!"

Ignoring Bugna, Bulan flew to the lake and dipped her feet. That same invigoration coursed through her body, making her feel more alive. She inhaled, welcoming her spirit. She embraced it, letting the two threads of life form a braid. Her thread of life had indeed thickened, but her goddess's spirit still burned through it, so she untangled the braid in a hurry. She let her body fall into the water, letting life seep back into her tired body.

She was too weak. She wished she had used anting-antings from a young age. Many people were going to die because she wasn't strong enough. Bugna pulled her out of the water. Even though her thread of life was still beating, Bugna panicked and checked her pulse.

"I'm fine, Mother," she said in a resigned voice. "Perhaps I chose the wrong body."

"Bulan—" Bugna dipped her head slightly, treating her differently from when she was just human.

"I'm going to keep my spirit in this body for a while. See if that helps."

"Not for a long time," Bugna said. "You could still banish your human soul without meaning to, just like souls from the afterlife trying to possess human beings. Only one spirit can reside in a body."

"I know that, Mother," Bulan said in a bored tone.

"You seem to have forgotten something," Bugna said. When Bulan stared at her blankly, Bugna raised an eyebrow. "We still have two bakunawa blades. Well, broken blades, to be exact. I've tried fixing them. They're nowhere near their original form because I didn't have time to collect the necessary anting-antings. Maybe you could do something." She grabbed her rattan bag and held it upside down. Broken pieces of the swords scattered on the ground. Bugna had managed to restore one blade to half its original length.

Bulan arranged the broken pieces into the complete shapes of the blades and added the tip that she'd been hiding in her pocket for a long time. Then she closed her eyes and, concentrating deeply, envisioned the blades in their original form. When she opened her eyes, the pieces remained broken. "Pieces of junk." She expelled her spirit. "Well, it looks like this half will have to do for now."

Bulan practiced with Bugna for the whole day. Bulan's thread of life grew stronger yet, and she tried to merge her spirits again the following day but failed. Even the half-broken blade needed some time to strengthen her.

"What about other demigods like you? Perhaps they'll listen," Bugna said the following day as they continued fighting.

"None remained here on earth," Bulan said, panting. "Bathala didn't want the revolution to reoccur. But..." She recalled others like her who'd chosen to stay on earth and died. "You're right. I can ask for their help."

Bugna vanished her magically conjured sword. "Then what are you waiting for?"

"It's not as easy as that. Unlike me and Bakunawa, it was a complete surrender. They can't use magic again because they weren't reborn. They chose to live as humans who died, and their souls are in the underworld. But perhaps... I can find their powers. Even if I could merge with my spirit, Kidlat is more powerful than me, but if I could gain my fellow demigods' powers..."

"You can defeat him. But where? How are you going to find them?" Bugna's voice rose with excitement.

"I don't know. But my sister, Tala, goddess of the stars, is in the afterlife. You can talk to souls, right?"

Bulan had one other sibling, Adlaw, god of the sun. She thought it ironic that her mortal brother shared the name. Adlaw chose to reside in the gods' realm. Even when the world was open to gods, he didn't like mingling with people. Tala, on the other hand, like Bulan, loved humans, perhaps more than Bulan did. She had chosen to live among them and to accept death.

Bugna raised both hands. "I don't have enough power to summon such a powerful soul. She could pull me to the afterlife without meaning to. You can talk to her instead."

"The afterlife is Dilim's domain. I can't reach it unless I go there physically. How about Linti, god of thunder? He was less powerful than Tala. He has a nasty temper, though. I'm worried about calling him."

"No." Bugna's forehead crunched in concentration. "Think, daughter. Not those gods closer to Bathala. We need those that are not well known." She pressed a thumb to her temple. "What now, Habagat?" When Bulan leaned closer in concern, Bugna held up a hand and mouthed, *I'm fine.* "Who? Didn't I tell you not to listen to my conversations unless I allowed it?" she told Datu Habagat. "Where? Fine."

Bugna's expression changed. She bowed deep.

When she finally stood straight, she didn't look Bulan in the eyes. "I, Datu Habagat, am humbled in your presence, Bulan, goddess of the moon and a great warrior."

"Nonsense. Why are you taking over Bugna's body?" Bulan backed away slowly, still wary of Datu Habagat's intentions.

"She... gave me permission so I could talk to you directly."

"Fine," Bulan said. "We've met before. Don't try to act nice now."

"I apologize for my previous attitude. I was consumed by hate for years."

"I've lived with humans for thousands of years. I'm used to your crude attitude. Get to the point. Why do you want to speak to me directly?" Bulan asked.

"I'm a direct descendant of a demigod."

Bulan cocked a head. "Who? And look at me." She wanted to look into his eyes, to see if he was lying.

"Bagyo, god of storms."

"And?"

"I know where his tomb is. It is a family treasure only the male heir knows. But no one has touched it. I'm sure I could wield the power, but I don't want to disrespect him."

"Bugna can summon him. Tell me where it is."

"I don't know the exact location, but here's what was passed on to me: 'Under the tree that is not a tree. Kissed by the sunshine, loathed by the sea. In your touch, I fold in shame.'"

Bulan nodded. She knew where that was.

"In my understanding, this was past Sulod, past the Bolo Warrior Barangay village in the south," Datu Habagat continued.

"Yes. A desert between the forests and the sea. We have to wait for the low tide."

"I have important information. Kidlat took Tago town. The news is spreading fast. Most of the pangayaws were killed—including Miguel—because they refused to join hands with him."

Bulan nodded in acknowledgement. She had wanted to kill Miguel herself for killing her father, Datu Bangkaw. The news didn't bring her the joy she'd expected.

"And... your mother is safe," Datu Habagat continued. "She's in the room where you and Makanas were—"

"Stop!" Bulan shouted. She knew Kidlat wouldn't find them unless someone opened the underground coated with the concealer. "Thank you. Let's call it even. In return for keeping them safe, I will not punish you for disrespecting me before."

Datu Habagat bowed and retreated from Bugna's body. With Bulan's help, Bugna exited the protection of the lake of life. Bulan had suggested that the shaman simply call Bagyo, and Bagyo would probably answer them, but Bugna insisted on following the ways of the shaman. Bulan built a table for the offerings. When the shaman returned, a cleaned wild boar floated behind her.

"Won't Kidlat find us if you cook?" Bulan asked.

"Yes. That's why I'm going to use shaman's fire." She murmured words of incantation, and fire erupted from her hands. In no time, they had roast meat on the ceremonial table.

"There are a lot of things missing, but I hope Bagyo will at least hear us." Bugna began her chant.

Bulan understood the words, which she never had before, for they were in an ancient tongue, the language of the gods.

The air shimmered of shiny dust blown by the wind. Then the air formed the shape of a man.

"Who dared to summon me?" the figure asked.

Wind howled outside the protection of the lake of life. The clouds swirled and gathered above them. The earth turned gloomy.

"Look who we have here," the man continued. "Bulan who's not Bulan. I was getting ready to punish this shaman. Thanks to you, she's spared."

"Same fickle Bagyo." Bulan sighed. "You were supposed to leave all your powers behind. Bathala won't be glad."

"Ah. Not my fault the wind and the clouds remember me. How interesting. It took you five thousand years to finally remember. It was frustrating to see how weak your mortal bodies were."

Bulan waved a hand to dismiss his words. "I need your help."

"What? Bulan? Daughter of the supreme ruler Bathala, goddess of war—"

"Enough!" Bulan screamed. "This is serious. It's not

a game you and other demigods crave. A second revolution might ensue."

"Fine. Fine. You get to shout, but I can't even talk. Anyway, what help?"

"I need to borrow your power."

"Not in the name of all the gods. It's reserved for my descendants." Bagyo's form started to fade.

"I've asked permission from Datu Habagat already." Bulan hid her smile as Bagyo's form became more prominent. "I'm only borrowing it to help me merge with my spirit."

"You know"—Bagyo cocked his head—"if you get all your powers back, you might be the reason for the second revolution."

Bulan's heart skipped a beat. Bagyo had a point. If she became powerful on earth, other demigods from the underworld might want to live too. Humans would get jealous of their powers again, and alliances would form. Wars would break out, culminating in a revolution against the gods just as when humans were at the peak of magic.

"I'm going to live and die as humans like you," she said. But that posed another problem. Her power, once left on earth, might fall into the wrong hands and enslave the rest of the people on earth. "Or stay in the gods' realm and abandon earth," she added.

"Good idea. Why don't you do just that after you merge with your mortal body?" Bagyo asked. "I highly doubt you would."

The Bolo Warrior

"I will. But first, I must resurrect Bakunawa," Bulan said with resolve.

"Poor Bakunawa," Bagyo said, glancing at Bakunawa lying in the lake of life. Bagyo and Bakunawa had been friends once. They rode the wind together, their laughter creating terror among human children. "Fine. For Bakunawa's sake."

14

UNA

Una swung her blade, and a man's head rolled to the side of the road. She kicked the body aside and strolled over to help Dasig, who was fighting two other warriors. She cursed. Datu Habagat was stupid to leave men behind. *Did he expect mercy from Kidlat?* Her blade found the warrior's belly. She twisted and looked the man in the eye.

"Don't resent me. This is better than seeing your body possessed by another soul." Una cringed as the man held her arm.

"Thank you," he managed to say as blood bubbled in his mouth.

Una kicked him, freeing her sword from his body. Not many men were left. Some had had the courage to take their own lives. Datu Habagat's once elegant house was smeared with blood and littered with dead bodies. The golden door was torn from its frame. She could almost picture a scene weeks from then, with rotting bodies lying around, and she almost gagged at the thought of the smell.

Una had expected Kidlat to punish her, but instead, he gave her the mission to find Amihan. At first, she'd thought the mission ridiculous, but she realized she'd been wrong. Kidlat had shown her that because of her actions, more lives were forfeit.

Warriors were entering countless rooms and leaving either empty-handed, or with food and gold. Kidlat needed as much gold and food for his growing army and as many slaves as they could find. Una didn't see Amihan, Adlaw, or even Liwayway. She wondered how many more lives she would have to end to find them. She left Datu Habagat's house to other warriors and climbed up into the huts of the datu's people. Most of them were empty, but she found some slaves possessed by souls.

Una was about to jump down the stairs of an empty hut when she sensed the slightest movement in a corner among three sacks of rice. She turned, barely dodging a knife thrown her way. Rice scattered on the floor and fell between the cracks. Standing on the sack that had fallen at their feet was a woman barely in her twenties and a boy about five or six years old.

The woman's hand shook, tears streaming down her face. "Just leave my son alone. You can kill me."

Una slowly brought the bolo blade down to her side. The mother posed no threat. The young boy was grasping two thin knives a few inches long. Una was worried he might hurt himself with them. He wasn't trembling like his mother, and Una wondered if the boy understood the danger they were in. Una didn't want to get closer, having learned that people sometimes acted unreasonably due to fear. She wanted them to feel a bit of safety with the distance between them.

"I'm not going to kill you," Una said though her words were wasted because the fear in the woman's eyes intensified and her hands continued to tremble. "Kidlat needs more workers."

"I'm good at planting rice," the woman said almost immediately. She dropped to her knees and touched the floor with her head. "I can teach my son. He's young, but he learns quick."

"Very well," Una said. "First, you must swear your allegiance to Kidlat." Una recited the prayer, saying the words loudly and slowly for the woman and her son to follow.

When everything was done, she stepped down the stairs, and the woman followed her. The boy remained at the door. His mother held out both hands to carry him, the four-step staircase allowing them to see eye to eye. The boy leaned forward and stabbed his mother in the throat.

Una moved without thinking, dodging as the boy hurled a blade at her throat. She seized the boy's arm and twisted it until the knife fell to the ground. "Why?" she growled at the boy.

"That woman thought I was ugly." The boy sneered.

"I don't think so. It's because you're too old."

Una realized she'd come too late and the boy had

been possessed for a while before they even reached Datu Habagat's barangay. She had noticed that souls took over the bodies of the children and the old first, or those who were sick.

The boy spat, but Una dodged by turning her head, which seemed to infuriate the soul possessing the boy. She knew she had to kill the boy, but she couldn't bring herself to do it. However, if the boy lived, he would suffer at the memory of having killed his own mother. She wondered if she could drive the soul out of the boy's body. She remembered Kidlat saying that the person's soul would wander as a lost spirit. Una thought she still had a chance. If she failed, she would leave the boy to fellow warriors who could stomach killing children.

Una looked into the boy's eyes. "You must be here. Listen to me. The only way to live is to recite the prayer again with your whole heart. You have to believe in it. Not just a pretense. You must accept Kidlat like he is your father. He is your datu. He isn't cruel like Habagat. He will save you. I didn't hurt you. He won't hurt you either. I promise you that." She ignored the words from the boy's mouth, spoken by an old man. Instead, she focused on the unseen, hoping the boy's soul was near and following along as she recited the prayer.

At first, the boy struggled against her more strongly than before. Then he screamed, reminding Una of a pig's cry when slaughtered, when the butcher's knife wasn't big enough to cut the neck in one strike. When he finally stopped screaming, he fell into Una's shoulders, hands limp. Not trusting the boy completely, she made sure his hands were always visible and tied him together with other slaves.

Mariit Inn was alive with lights and noises when Una's troop returned to Tago town that night. Soldiers assigned slaves to head attendants. Prostitutes with unnaturally white faces laughed with the warriors. A few pangayaws were stacking stones around the inn. Kidlat was apparently building a stone wall there. Una noted how tumandoks, her people, treated the foreign pangayaws harshly, even when they were all slaves. The tables had turned.

Occasional cries from the slave women shattered the merry environment as warriors forced them into tents surrounding the inn, occupied by Kidlat's best fighters. Residents near the inn were driven out, their stone houses given to Kidlat's head attendants and their new slaves. Some remained and promised to offer half of their income to the new ruler.

Una's eyelids felt heavy. Her sore muscles demanded rest, and her clothes, damp from the afternoon rain, were musty, but she waited for the evening prayer. To ensure the people were safe from souls, they had enforced a morning and evening prayer for everyone. Baskog stood on the veranda of the second floor of the inn, leading the prayer.

Kidlat had been missing for days, searching for Linay. He had instructed each of the flying warriors to search as well, except Una, whose mission was to find Amihan. Kidlat didn't seem to need protection except when he was sleeping. Each day, more and more shamans surrendered to Kidlat, making him even more powerful. Some powerful shamans who didn't want to join hands with Kidlat were either killed or imprisoned in the underground ring of the Mariit Inn.

She headed to her tent after the prayer and undid the tie of her sword. As one of the higher ranked air warriors, Una had her own small tent, barely big enough to cover her from head to foot to give her some privacy. Other warriors slept together or rested on the cold floor of the inn. As she entered her tent, she jumped at seeing a man inside. Her shoulders drooped with relief as she realized it was only Dasig. Dasig held her gaze and, without a word, kissed her passionately. They made love, her moans masked by the bustling noise outside. Dasig, as always, was passionate but never rough with her. He lay beside her afterward, watching the rise and fall of her stomach.

Dasig leaned closer and kissed her neck. Una was thankful the rain had washed the blood and some of the grime from her skin, but she wished she'd taken a bath.

"Makanas is alive," Dasig whispered.

Una sat up straight. "Where?"

Dasig sat up and touched her arm, which was irritating. *This isn't a time for more touching.* She needed answers, but then she realized Dasig wasn't just touching her. His index finger moved against her skin, writing letters. Una understood and wrote back, touching his arm and writing in response. They both lay awake through the night, sharing strategies. Una was at peace that their relationship had been revealed to the other warriors before Bakunawa rose. They hadn't batted an eye when Dasig entered her tent, and the two of them could communicate whenever they wanted to without suspicion. They finally slept at the first crow of the roosters.

Una visited Iyay in her room in the inn the following morning. The old woman seemed to have aged a decade since they arrived in town. Her eyes and cheeks were hollower. Her vision was unfocused. No healer or shaman could heal her, for her illness wasn't physical. Una broke the news to her but warned she must show no sign, or Kidlat would know Makanas was alive. Iyay promised to stay in her room as she had always done since they arrived, and to eat little. They decided to communicate through tracing letters on their arms too, fearing warriors with enhanced hearing might hear them. In this way, Iyay gave Una the names and locations of the shamans she knew.

Una insisted on searching for Amihan alone after her visit to Iyay. The warriors assigned to her didn't mind. Kidlat was allowing them freedom, at least for a few days, as a reward for defending the Bolo Warrior Barangay. She decided to visit Tanda first. Makanas had told her Tanda could see the future. Una had only heard rumors about Tanda, but Dasig had told her last night he might be their strongest ally if Kidlat hadn't killed him yet.

She found Tanda in the yard of his two-story stone house, yelling in frustration as his gamecock fell to the ground. The poor white rooster's leg shivered as blood pooled around it, its white feathers making the blood seem all the more red in contrast. The judge started counting. At the count of three, the rooster stood and limped.

"Yes!" Tanda roared with joy. "White!"

Others echoed him, but those shouting "Red!" were louder. The shouting continued, as if their cheering actually affected the fight between the two roosters.

Una stood unnoticed, wondering how people could gamble during a time of war. The crowd dispersed as soon as the cockfight ended. Tanda's yard emptied out except for Una.

"Unless you came with coconut wine, you're not welcome," Tanda said. He gawked at Una. His lanky frame made Una doubt he was the same man who'd fought and saved Makanas and Dasig.

Una opened her bag and handed him a bottle of coconut wine and a tobacco leaf. "I stole this last night. The coconut wine is a bit sour now."

Tanda waved a hand, signaling Una to follow him into his house. He sat cross-legged in his bare living room without offering Una anything. If Una had indeed been there for a visit, his actions would've been considered rude.

"What game do you want to play?" he asked.

The Bolo Warrior

"I'm not here to gamble."

But Una realized she was indeed there to gamble, for if Tanda told Kidlat about her visit, she could be executed. She couldn't return to the inn without asking for help either. She could count on her fingers the number of warriors she could trust. Una needed help and was about to tell Tanda about Makanas when the tall man stood and disappeared into the kitchen.

Alone in the living room, Una listened for any sign of life from the rest of the house but couldn't hear anything. Even the street in front of the house was empty.

Tanda returned with a roll of paper, a brush, and a cauldron of charcoal. He unrolled the paper and wrote in small strokes, *Makanas is alive.*

Una stopped herself from gasping. She accepted the brush and replied under Tanda's writing. *We know. And we need your help. I need you to find these shamans who could help Makanas and defeat the new ruler.* She wrote the names of the shamans Iyay had given her.

Tanda stared at the names for a long time, frowning from time to time. Una moved to sit beside the man, eager to communicate more quickly without passing the paper across the floor.

First, you must free Putot, Tanda wrote. When she shot him a questioning look, he explained how Putot, a shaman, could put a tracker on someone to control them.

Tanda explained that Putot was a descendant of the banished shamans and had been born in Yungib, a cave between the afterlife and the world of the living. The banished shamans were the most powerful shamans thousands of years before, when humans waged wars against the gods. Bathala banished them from the land of the living. Some of them had escaped before they could turn into beasts.

Una realized then that the beasts they'd fought in Sulod had once been those powerful shamans. Putot's power wasn't gained from anting-antings but inherited. She carried dark magic from the afterlife. With her tracker, essentially a poison from her bite when she turned into a snake, souls would think a person was already dead, so they would avoid possessing those who had her tracker. Tanda explained further that Putot might have not realized the power she had, for she was only about a thousand years old.

Una grabbed the brush and the paper and wrote, *Then how did you know about this if Putot didn't even know about it?*

Tanda's appearance changed to that of an old man. His hair turned white, and deep wrinkles lined his face. *Because I was also one of the banished.* When Una blinked, his appearance changed back to the body of a forty-year-old man.

Una returned to the inn before noon, and Tanda followed her. He turned into a skinny young boy and kept his head low most of the time. They passed through the gate without questions. Most guards knew Una, and those who were new didn't guard the gate without a senior. They headed to Una's tent, where Tanda changed his appearance into Una.

"You got all the details, old man." Una exclaimed, circling Tanda. "Down to the scar on my toe."

"Back off, woman," Tanda said with a sneer, sounding exactly like Una. He grabbed her weapons roughly and left.

Inside her tent, Una paced. They'd hoped Putot would recognize Tanda and would go with him right away. She wanted to go down to the underground ring herself and bring Putot out, but Tanda had pointed out that she would fail because she didn't have a smooth tongue. He also said he'd seen the future and he wasn't simply guessing what would happen if she tried to rescue Putot.

Her tent flap opened, and she sprang into action, immediately disarming the intruder then pinning him facedown with a knee. "Who sent you?"

The man grunted. "No one." He was young, probably younger than Una.

She pinned him harder with her weight and pressed a knife against his neck.

"I was just hoping to steal an anting-anting. I saw you went out."

Now I have to kill this boy. "What do you know about my anting-anting?"

"I don't know. People say it makes you strong."

"Why me?"

"Be-because you're a woman."

Una slapped the back of his head. "Is that weaker than a man's slap?"

"No. Please let me go. I'm sorry."

Una could feel the boy trembling. She would really get angry if he pissed in her tent. She'd paid a high price when she hesitated to kill someone before. And if Tanda returned with her face on, things would get complicated. "I'll help you hunt for anting-antings later." Una stood and let the young warrior rise to his feet. "But come here again, and you'll die."

The young man bolted. Una opened the flap of her tent ever so slightly to make sure he didn't linger. Her mind raced, still questioning herself for letting the warrior go.

Tanda came out of the inn later, Putot following her with her head down. Mimi wasn't with her. Una was so used to the shaman riding her giant cat that, at first, she thought Putot was just a child. A warrior spoke to Tanda, who was able to dismiss the man so easily that Una thought Tanda had an anting-anting to charm people into believing whatever he said.

Just as Una had done with Dasig, she traced letters against Putot's arm to share their plan. The shaman was a bit skeptical, but she turned into a snake. Una closed her eyes and waited for the snake's fangs to penetrate her skin. It didn't hurt as much as she'd imagined. The pain was just amplified by her fear. Once it was over, Putot proceeded to plant another tracker on Tanda.

Tanda left the inn after the changing of the guard, while Una stayed in her tent the whole day. She couldn't go out until the next change. She hoped they would find Makanas soon. And she hoped Makanas was strong enough to join hands with Bulan and overthrow Kidlat. In the meantime, she brainstormed how to tell a believable story about how Putot had escaped.

15

THE CHANTER

Bugna and Bulan flew south at night, past the vast desert, to the sea. Datu Habagat had told them Kidlat, even with Bakunawa's power, was still a man and usually spent nights at Mariit Inn, but he hadn't returned for days. Bulan had left all her anting-antings in the lake of life, fearing Kidlat's detection.

Bulan stood on a rock, waiting for low tide. She let go of her spirit, worried that her mortal thread of life would snap from being in constant contact with it.

When the tide finally ebbed, she let her spirit in and flew over the water, looking for anything resembling a tree. She found an umbrella-shaped rock. Bagyo had once showed his prowess by shaping a rock into a tree merely using the forces of wind, rain, and waves. That was the tree that wasn't a tree, which he'd mentioned in his message to his descendants. Bulan swam over and confirmed that it was indeed the same tree. Then Bulan had to find the *makahiya* plant, whose leaves folded at the slightest touch. Bagyo's choice to decorate his tomb with such a plant didn't make sense, but Bulan didn't question. That was just Bagyo being unpredictable. He'd told her just to travel straight from the rock tree to the desert.

Bagyo had warned her, too, that she couldn't obtain his power with her spirit. Before he died, he'd made sure demigods couldn't steal his power. Bulan expelled her spirit as she spotted the makahiya plants. Bugna flew behind her, watching her back.

Carefully, she pulled the makahiya plants one by one, making a path to walk on. The thorny plants folded at her touch. Bulan was patient but also anxious that Kidlat might spot them. She stopped when she stepped on a rock. She cleared the sand off it and found it had an ancient inscription in the words of the gods: *He who seeks power without a heart will fail.*

Bulan sighed. "Here we are again with cryptic messages."

Bagyo hadn't given them a warning. The demigods loved leaving cryptic messages just to fool around with humans. Bulan loved playing with words, but what she didn't like was that clues were normally only known to other demigods. She bent down to lift the white stone. The three-foot-wide stone looked flat, and Bulan thought it wouldn't be hard to get it out of the way.

She stopped. To her right in the sand was a black stone the shape of a heart. She snatched it, put into a pocket, and lifted the rock again. The earth seemed to crumble beneath her. Bugna became farther and farther away, and the sand followed Bulan as she plummeted. She was about to call her spirit back but remembered Bagyo had warned her against that. Bugna tried to fly down, but the sand formed a roof and shut the earth close above Bulan.

She crashed against a marble floor, sand all over her body. "Bagyo really loves chaos," she muttered to herself. She rose to her feet and looked for any sign of bones. She knew better than to get tricked again, so she gathered some sand together to mark where she'd landed. Even though the roof was made of sand, it didn't collapse. The walls were made of white marble producing white light, which reminded Bulan of the gods' realm. She had only two choices: either move forward, or follow the hall backward. No signs were nearby to help her. She cursed Bagyo in her mind then scolded herself for cursing. Amihan hadn't allowed her to curse, but she was no longer a binukot. She could curse all she wanted, but it still felt wrong. Bagyo would pay for making her work so hard.

She decided to move forward. Walking seemed too slow for her, making her more frustrated, but she didn't want to call back her spirit, not until she got a hold of Bagyo's bones. She walked on and on for hours. She wondered if she had wasted her time by coming, but she knew she would waste more time if she returned without a more powerful magic. She hoped Bugna would find a way in and help speed her journey.

When she saw the end of the path, she ran. It was just a wall. She wondered if she'd chosen the wrong path. Perhaps she should go back and see where the opposite path led. She sat to massage her aching feet. Her mortal body frustrated her.

She noticed a spot on the floor. The small indentation was completely black and shaped like a heart.

The stone! She pressed a hand against her pocket. She sighed, thankful for the button keeping the stone inside. The heart must be the key. With a steady hand, she fitted the heart-shaped stone against the floor. A creaking sound made her heart beat quickly.

You sneak, Bagyo. I'm going to have your power. A few feet away, a part of the floor collapsed. She ran to see Bagyo's bones, but nothing but darkness lay below. She crouched closer to see and cursed as the floor collapsed underneath her. She landed on soft sand, to her relief. The sand sparkled, lighting the surroundings, as though Bulan's presence was welcome. She looked up, and found that the only way for her to get back was to fly. She turned to see that behind her was just a wall made of sand. The only way would be to move forward. Just like the marble hall above her, the hall she was in was bare. Before she could even get to her feet, the sand moved and rose into the figure of a man.

"I've come with Bagyo's permission. Show me his remains." Wondering if her words had been rude, she stood and bowed her head.

The thing, which Bulan decided to call a sandman, just stared at her with two hollow eyes. She wondered if it would stay still when Bulan passed. She decided to test it. She turned sideways to fit between the sandman and the wall. It moved, blocking her way. She pushed harder. The sandman was as strong as a rock.

"I am Bulan, goddess of the moon and war. You will let me pass." She was running out of patience.

She backed away and ran to kick it. It collapsed, only to form into a sandman again, but the sandman didn't retaliate. Apparently, its goal was simply to stop Bulan. She wondered how to fight something that couldn't get hurt. She tried fighting again by running away and returning with a kick. That was when she noticed that its feet stayed on the ground. Even when it walked, it dragged its feet. It seemed to need constant contact with the floor.

If I could only fly now. But all her anting-antings were back in the lake of life. She looked around for any clue that would help her defeat the sandman, and noticed the wall on her right was darker in color, like the sand had been wet.

"I'm sorry," she said, "but you're going to be washed away."

She dug the darker colored sand with her bare hands. She dug faster and faster until cold water started flowing in. The wall collapsed. The ceiling crumbled. Water filled the passageway. She closed her eyes against the pain of the salt water and struggled to breathe, flinging her arms about. She needed to break the surface before she lost consciousness. She took a big gulp of air when she finally reached the surface.

A few feet away was the tree that wasn't a tree. "It doesn't make sense," she said to herself. She looked back, wondering if she'd indeed chosen the wrong path, then the tree started to rise. Under the tree, stone roots held an earthen jar in place. Bulan swam toward it, wary of any tricks Bagyo might have prepared.

"So you found me." Bagyo laughed, floating alongside Bugna as they also approached the tree.

"You came back?" Bulan was burning with rage but tried to hide it, lest Bagyo change his mind.

"I never left. I wanted to see if that mortal body is indeed deserving. Well done. No more surprises." He shrugged.

Bugna was silent. Bulan looked for any warning sign from the shaman about any danger from the jar, but she couldn't read the shaman's expression. She opened the jar and found Bagyo's bones. She realized she had a problem. Without her anting-antings, she didn't know which one contained his power. Maybe she could pick any one, but Bagyo's mischievousness made that unlikely. She wondered what would happen if she chose a wrong bone. Bulan racked her brain. *What body part was Bagyo's favorite?* For a moment, she was tempted to ask for his help, but she knew Bagyo, and he would likely mislead her. She took a deep breath to clear her mind and drive away her anger. She had come far and wouldn't let her anger cripple her.

"What are you waiting for? My power is just a touch away." Bagyo sounded just like he had been as a mortal when they first came to earth—no hint of malice. That was why he was so good at deception. Bulan remembered the times when Bagyo cleared the skies just before the strongest storm.

Bulan bent and grabbed Bagyo's index finger. She rose into the air, wind swirling around her as though she was in the eye of a tornado.

"Calm down!" Bagyo screamed.

"How dare you!" Bulan growled as the wind strengthened around her. "You knew Bakunawa's mortal body could die. You knew Dilim could rule the earth without other gods caring."

"You're going to kill humans! I'm sorry," Bagyo said. "I needed to know you could handle my power. If you're weak, humans could take it away from you."

Bugna raised a hand, and the wind around Bulan settled to a light breeze. "Bagyo was right. I know you're strong, but it's his power."

"You knew?" Bulan asked in a raised tone.

"Only after you fell down that hole. And I couldn't help anyway. I couldn't break the spell Bagyo had laid there."

"I'm going to help you," Bagyo said. "As long as you hold my power, I'll be your companion, just like how normal shamans have powerful soul companions."

Bulan rolled her eyes. "I don't need you. All I have to do is return to the lake of life and merge my soul and spirit." And if she succeeded, she would regain her remaining power, which was locked in the moon.

Bugna wrung her hands, which she seemed to do when in deep thought or something was bothering her.

Then she massaged her temples, like she was having a headache. "I'm afraid we can't do that."

"Why not? I can practice with Bagyo's power there, and my thread of life is stronger there. It's the most sensible place to merge with my spirit."

"Kidlat has finally figured out where it is."

"Bakunawa!" Bulan's mind raced. "What if he kills Bakunawa?"

"He won't dare cross the barrier. Bakunawa's power is weak there. Habagat told me Kidlat's waiting for our return just outside the lake of life."

"You're faster than him!" Bulan said but realized Bugna could not enter the lake of life of her own will.

"Bagyo," Bugna said, "I need you to look like Bulan. Let Kidlat capture me."

"I don't have power anymore," Bagyo said.

"Let me worry about that. You said that the wind remembers you."

"Yes, but... Kidlat might be able to tell I'm a soul."

Bugna looked at Bulan from head to foot. "Take your clothes off."

Bulan instinctively crossed her arms. "What?"

16

UNA

Una soon tired of the celebration, but the warriors seemed to love it, and since Kidlat still hadn't returned, they continued drinking and enjoying the company of women. The last morning Kidlat was there, he'd told them this would be a special occasion when he allowed his warriors to indulge in vices. He'd told them to drink as much as they could because after he took Bulan's power, they would have to go to war again. Una wondered what kind of war it would be as nobody dared to harm Kidlat's warriors. His power had spread from town to town and city to city.

Una jumped as an arm circled her waist. "I told you not to do that when I'm not looking." She let her blade fall back into its scabbard.

"Sorry," Dasig muttered. "Let's go."

Una followed him. She tried her best not to punch the men who looked at them with teasing eyes.

"Hey, man! Tent's too small for you?" One guard teased as they passed through the front gate. "We prefer it if you do it here."

Dasig nodded at him, which irritated even Una more. He could've simply said something to shut the man up.

She inched closer to Dasig and held his arm. "We don't want anyone listening to every breath we take."

The guards laughed but ignored her. "Get it tonight, man!" the same guard teased. "Work all day and all night. Bet you'll be tired tomorrow."

"Shut up!" Una turned her head. "Go get some prostitutes, will you?"

"Stop wasting your time," Dasig said.

"What I don't understand is why you're still letting them walk all over you. You could kill them with a punch. Show them their place."

"They're not the enemy. Keep your voice down."

"Fine," Una grumbled as they turned a corner. "This is the wrong route."

"Sorry. You lead the way."

"You mean you haven't been there?"

"No."

"Then how did you know about him?"

"I told you he helped us before. And... someone else told me more about him."

"Who?"

"You'll know when we get there."

Tanda's house was quiet when they arrived. Dinner

time was past, and even the lamps were unlit. The door opened before they could knock.

"We have an empty room," To anyone who might be looking, Tanda seemed like a lucky man to welcome paying travelers despite the chaos in town. He closed the door after them, led them to a small room, and pulled a slab of stone aside, revealing a staircase to the underground. Anting-anting orbs of light hung to the sides of the stairs. He pulled on another slab and motioned for Una and Dasig to enter.

"What about you?" Una asked.

She didn't trust the man. He might lock them down there and sell them out to Kidlat.

"I'm waiting for one more," Tanda said.

Dasig nodded and stepped down the stairs. "Come on."

Una followed with hesitant steps. At first, she heard murmurs, then the only thing she could hear were their own footsteps against the stone stairs. When they finally reached the bottom of the stairs, about twenty people were sitting cross-legged on a mat in a circle, and all eyes were on them. Putot was sitting among them and waved for them to come over. Una's gaze stopped at a girl sitting next to Putot.

"What are you doing here? Get back to the inn this instant," Una said, approaching Kayay.

"I have my father's permission," Kayay said in a small but steady voice.

"Let her be. She'll be helpful," Dasig said. "Warriors won't suspect a child."

"Still..." Una backed away as she spotted Datu Habagat leaning against the wall. "What is he doing here? You can't trust this man."

"He's the only one who can talk to Bugna and Lin-ay."

Una turned to the stairs and saw Head Guard Uwak behind Tanda. She bowed, and the head guard nodded in acknowledgment.

"We're all here," Tanda said.

The people repositioned themselves, expanding the circle. Datu Habagat joined them.

As Dasig sat to her left, Una sat next to Putot. "First, you must make sure they're safe," she told her.

"They're all done except for him"—Putot nodded toward Dasig—"and Head Guard Uwak."

"I swore an oath. I'm safe," Dasig said.

"No, you're not," Tanda said. "You're not devoted to Kidlat. It'll be only a matter of time before a stronger soul gets to you. When they kill their weak host, they'll get stronger and will find a stronger host like you."

Putot turned into a snake and slithered toward Head Guard Uwak, who didn't even blink when the snake's fangs disappeared into his skin.

"It doesn't hurt," Una said.

She squeezed Dasig's hand as the snake's head poised to strike. He didn't even close his eyes but released a breath when it was finally over.

Putot almost fell to the ground when she transformed back. "I must have used a lot of my power today. The room's spinning."

Una held her hand and helped her back to her seat.

"Before we talk about anything else, there's an urgent matter you need to know," Datu Habagat said. "Kidlat has located Lin-ay's hiding place—"

"Wait!" Una raised a hand. "What if people with anting-antings can hear us?"

"They can't," Tanda said. "This room is protected by a concealer. It can't be detected."

"Just like the prison in the Bolo Warrior Barangay?" Una asked.

"Yes," Putot confirmed.

"We need to stop Kidlat from killing Lin-ay," Dasig said.

"Bugna will try to set some bait," Datu Habagat said. "If she fails, she might need our help to create some distractions."

"Where is this hiding place?" Tanda asked, hand on his knee.

"That's another problem," Datu Habagat said. "I know the name, but I don't know where it is. She said it's the lake of life."

"I know where it is!" Tanda said immediately. "But even with your ability to fly, it would be too late for us to stop Kidlat. It takes at least six days for those who can fly."

"That means we have six days here without Kidlat," Putot said.

Tanda bobbed his head. "Or less. He has Bakunawa's power. He's stronger and faster than anyone alive. In the meantime, we could gather those with stronger anting-antings. Humans used to rival the demigods. With combined powers—"

"But we must keep Makanas alive!" Dasig said. His tone was surprising because he normally just listened. But he and Makanas had been friends since they were young.

"He's right," Datu Habagat said. "We must save my son first."

"Your son?" Una asked. Her words echoed in the room. So that was why Datu Habagat had killed Dungog. Una hadn't understood that move.

Datu Habagat raised a hand. "I'm talking to Bugna now."

The room went quiet, and tension rose as everyone waited.

"Thanks be to the good spirits. And Bagyo? Good, good." Datu Habagat nodded absently as he talked to Bugna. "We'll distract him so you can get back. Yes, yes. And Makanas? Th-thank you, Bugna."

"What did she say?" Dasig asked. "Is Makanas safe?"

"Yes, but not for long. Bugna and Lin-ay tried to get back into the lake of life, but they were unable. Thankfully, they escaped Kidlat's trap."

"But what happened to Makanas? Why did he fall down like that when Bakunawa died?" Una asked.

Datu Habagat released a long sigh. "I also didn't know this before, but... Makanas is Bakunawa."

Una couldn't help but laugh. "I appreciate the

humor, Datu." Thinking Datu Habagat had perhaps gone insane, she glanced around and saw shamans looking uncomfortable.

They, too, seemed to think the datu's words were ridiculous, except Tanda, who nodded for him to continue.

Datu Habagat, unfazed by the crowd's reaction, stared at the wall as he continued. "He's my son, and I must save him." He told everybody how Makanas had fallen into Kidlat's hands, and he shared Kidlat's plan to have Makanas kill Datu Habagat, his own father. He also told them that Makanas and Bakunawa were once one, a demigod, but he was broken into two. His human soul was reborn as a man, but his spirit was trapped in a serpent's body.

Una stared at the ground, not laughing anymore. The revelation was hard to process. Lin-ay being possessed by Bulan was easier for her to understand, but Makanas... They'd trained together since she was nine. She saw how hard he'd tried and failed to awaken the bakunawa blade. "Bakunawa is dead. Then Makanas—"

"Is still alive," Datu Habagat said. "The lake of life extends his life, but not for long because his soul was sucked in the snare ball. Lin-ay must merge with Bulan. Then she would be strong enough to fight Kidlat and then recover both Makanas's soul and spirit."

"If my memory serves me right," Tanda said, "Bulan is more powerful than Bakunawa."

"Yes, but Kidlat has five bakunawa blades. Four were fused into one."

"Ah. How unfortunate. That puts her at a disadvantage. But if she indeed succeeds in merging with her spirit, she'll get her power back from the moon."

"Yes. She should be able to merge with her spirit now, but she said it needs to be done in the lake of life, the doorway to the gods' realm. Our powers combined aren't strong enough to get Kidlat's attention. We can try after freeing the imprisoned shamans at Mariit Inn, but I doubt it's enough. You saw what happened when I tried to fight Kidlat last time." Datu Habagat nodded toward Dasig and Una.

"We have no time to hunt anting-antings now," Una said.

"Not anting-antings," Datu Habagat said. "We're fighting a demigod. That's why I specifically made sure you're no longer loyal to Kidlat, Una."

"Me?" Una raised an eyebrow. "Don't tell me I'm also a demigod."

"You're not, but one of your ancestors is."

A collective gasp seemed to suck the air out of the underground. Dasig's hand gripped Una's, and she let out a nervous laugh.

"Impossible. I was barren. I couldn't even use an anting-anting when I was young. And what if my ancestor is a demigod? That has nothing to do with me." But at the back of her mind, she could hear a shaman's chant she remembered from when she was young. The chant included names of their ancestors long dead, powerful shamans and datus who guided the living, as well as a demigod.

"It's important," Tanda said, "because that means you can absorb the demigod's magic directly into your body, just like Datu Habagat. If you succeed, Kidlat couldn't detect you."

Una tried to remember the name of the demigod, but all she could hear was the melody of the chant. "Who's the demigod? And what should I do?"

Tanda revealed the demigod's name, and explained to Una what should be done. The meeting went on until midnight. Head Guard Uwak assured everyone that he would make sure the guards wouldn't notice the shamans' disappearance from the underground and that he would kill any guard that might pose a problem. The shamans dispersed, each aiming to be more powerful before Kidlat returned. Only Dasig and Una remained at Tanda's house. Tanda killed his gamecocks for an offering.

"What kind of shaman gambles and cheats?" Una asked as she placed a whole boiled chicken on the table.

"I only cheat with cheaters, giving them a dose of their own medicine." Tanda placed betel nut chew and a pitcher of coconut wine on the right side of the table. "Hurry and bring all the chicken. We have to finish quickly. You need to get some rest before we set out tomorrow."

They finished setting the table with a few trips back

and forth to the kitchen. Dasig, who looked exhausted, guarded the door and made sure no one approached the house while the ceremony was going on.

Tanda chanted for a long time, his brow furrowed and his hands clasped in concentration. Despite his clear voice and the appealing offering, the soul he summoned didn't show its presence. He paused and held out a hand. "I think Linog doesn't think of me as a worthy shaman. I need a drop of your blood." He lit a candle and put it on the ceremonial table.

Una pulled a knife strapped to her leg and pricked her forefinger. She held her hand over the candle and let her blood drip.

Tanda continued his chant. "Oh, Linog, the great god of earthquake, I implore you to please lend us your ears. Forgive us for disturbing your peace."

The table trembled. The house shook. Una's first concern was people leaving their houses and finding them doing a ceremony. Tanda wasn't the least concerned despite the shaking of the plates. Una held the table to keep it steady.

"How interesting."

The voice confused Una, for it definitely sounded like hers. She looked up to see who it was and jumped back from a face that looked exactly like hers.

"I was sure she was barren." The soul knelt and touched Una's face as the side of her mouth turned up in a smirk. "How did this thing become so powerful?"

"I…" Una cleared her throat and cursed herself for sounding like a frog. "I trained with Kidlat."

"Hmm. When I saw you for the first time, I thought I would give you my power, but you couldn't even make an anting-anting work. I'm at peace in the underworld. I thought I'd give up on waiting for a descendant who could wield my power."

"We are humbled in your presence, Linog. Thank you so much for hearing us." Tanda bowed his head low.

"You're still alive, Tanda. Did you just let your anting-anting rot for thousands of years?" Linog asked.

"I've spent my time preparing all these years, Goddess of the Earthquake."

Linog snorted. "But you still managed to stay weak."

"Yes, I am lacking in so many ways, but your descendant here, I believe, can be powerful enough to help Bulan."

"Hmm. I've never been a shaman's companion. But I would like to try, to see how it feels to walk the earth," Linog said as though Una wasn't in the room with them. "But... I can't send my descendant on a quest that might kill her. She doesn't even have a child yet. If she dies, it'll be the end of my lineage."

"I'm not going to die. Please, give me your power." Una hated to beg, but she'd only just learned that she even had the chance to gain a demigod's power. "If I don't try to help Bulan, I might die anyway. I've already betrayed Kidlat. No way is he going to let me live."

After much persuasion, Linog finally agreed, but getting her power wasn't as simple as Una had thought.

Linog told her of the traps she'd set for anyone who sought her power. Una, determined, brushed off the warning. She didn't care if she died. She would die trying. Tanda forced her and Dasig to sleep for a few hours, but everything she'd learned in the last days kept her awake.

If Makanas was a demigod, he could surely defeat Kidlat once he was awake. But then she remembered Lin-ay's failure to control Bulan. *What if Makanas acts like a lunatic because he can't control his spirit?* The concept of a soul and a spirit together in one body was even more confusing. *How can a demigod have two personas after the split?*

Dasig snored loudly. Una wanted to smack him.

"Dear spirits," she huffed.

She loved him but hated how loud he was when he slept. She nudged him a bit, and he stopped. The moment she closed her eyes, he snored again, louder. Una sat up. Dasig's peaceful face irritated her all the more. She vowed to have a separate room built when they married and perhaps to seal it with clay to avoid hearing his snoring. For that night, she decided to try sleeping in the living room and rose quietly despite her frustration.

When she saw a figure in the living room, she drew her blade. After a few blinks, she realized it was only Linog. "I thought souls aren't supposed to wander in the land of the living."

"What's the use of that now?" Linog asked, sitting

cross-legged like a normal person. "Most of the evil souls are out. Besides, my stay here is granted. Tanda summoned me, so I'm still following the rules of the afterlife. And... if you succeed in getting my power, I can stay here longer, just like Iyay's companion."

"Ah. I forgot about that," Una said.

Iyay did indeed have a powerful companion from the afterlife whom she called for help and asked about things she didn't know.

"But I'm not a shaman. I don't know anything about shaman's ceremonies and such."

"Eh. Those are just nonsense. Shamans without strong connections to the afterlife need to be good with words, beg, and flatter the souls with adorations, or else they won't listen. You have me."

Una nodded. She'd thought she was past the stage of doubting herself. In the past couple years, she had grown confident, sure of herself. But she cared only about her personal achievements back then. She had wanted to be Makanas's most trusted warrior, along with Dasig, when Makanas ascended as the head warrior. But presently, too much was at stake.

Linog must have sensed her unease, for she disappeared into the kitchen and came back with a cup. "Drink this."

She noticed the smell of the sleeping potion later, when her eyes were already closing. Later, she woke to the sound of Tanda's grumbling.

"I don't allow thieves in the house," Tanda said,

smelling the cup on the table where Una had put it before she fell asleep.

"It wasn't that hard to collect." Una rubbed the sleep off her eyes then dragged her bottom across the floor as she reached for her bag. "Here, old man!"

Tanda caught the vial midair. "You could've taken this instead. Why steal mine?"

"Linog tricked me." Una didn't like drinking sleeping potions. She feared something might happen while she slept.

Linog had left without a trace, perhaps hiding from Tanda after stealing the potion. Una hadn't known souls could touch things.

"Hurry and get prepared. Just eat breakfast on the way."

"There's nothing to prepare," Una said and looked down at her blouse. "I have all I need. Are you going with us?"

"No," Tanda said. "I must free the shamans in the underground. By now, Putot must have finished injecting them all with trackers." He packed smoked meat and some dried fruits and shoved them into Una's bag. "Linog is enough to guide you."

"How do I summon her? I can't see her."

"She's here. Just call her name. She's my companion for now, so she could stay here in the land of the living. Once you get her power, I will sever my ties with her, and she should be able to choose you as a companion." Tanda pushed Una's bag toward her. "You must recover Linog's power at all costs, but be careful, and make sure you follow us to the lake of life. Linog knows where it is. We will most likely fail without you."

"Don't rely on me too much, old man." Una slung her bag over one shoulder. In a lower voice, she added, "But I'll try to do my best. In the meantime, keep Makanas and Lin-ay alive."

Una and Dasig headed west. Linog had told them the previous night that his tomb was in Una's father's barangay. Tanda had also told them that the lake of life was to the west, opposite the gate to the afterlife to the east. Una was planning to head to the lake of life after getting Linog's power without going back to town.

Her father's barangay was on top of a mountain, a two-week walk from Tago town. Una hadn't been there for years. The last time she'd visited was when she killed her cousin. Then the barangay collapsed under her traitorous uncle's rule. His greed had left the barangay's defense weak, and the people under his rule abandoned him and joined other barangays. To Una, the downfall started when her father died. According to some who had passed by the mountain, nature had taken over. The only traces remaining of the once rich barangay were tombstones decorated with sculptures of the dead.

They reached the barangay in two days. The people's description was right. It was just a mountain, not a barangay. Flying here and there, she couldn't even pinpoint where their house had once stood until she spotted the balete tree, its roots hanging from the lower branches like curtains. She recalled her happy childhood spent climbing the tree and swinging through those roots.

Dasig held her hand, and Una squeezed back, grateful that his warmth chased away her dark memories.

17

THE CHANTER

"Let go. You're going to kill yourself." Bugna held Bulan's arm tightly.

Bulan didn't want to let go of her spirit. Bugna could travel from one place to another in a blink, but Kidlat was fast, and he could sense Bagyo's power. She had yet to learn how to use Bagyo's power. Once, she'd summoned a wind that smacked them against a rock.

Bugna had told her that the only way to hide the power was to absorb it completely into her body, but they didn't have enough time to do that, and Bugna was too weak to do the ceremony. Also, Bulan wasn't confident that her mortal body could handle it. She was terrified that Kidlat would catch up to them while she was still vulnerable. Besides, she still didn't know if extracting the power later and giving it to Datu Habagat was possible. Bulan thought Kidlat was arrogant for coming after them alone. Perhaps he thought his warriors were just a nuisance. Bulan was thankful that he had no access to Bakunawa's memories, or he would know that Bulan hesitated to kill humans and could use that to his advantage.

"Now, Bulan. Let go now, or I'll leave you to fight Kidlat." Bugna shook Bulan's shoulders as if trying to wake her up.

Slowly, Bulan expelled her spirit and felt her body weaken. Bugna had been right. Her thread of life had almost burned. She struggled to even keep her body straight as she floated. The wind threw her head back as Bugna transported them again to another place. They'd been there before and seemed to be going in circles. She realized that even though Bugna was fast, she couldn't jump from one side of the planet to another at once. And although the shaman was strong, traveling took a toll on her. Her once shiny hair had grown disheveled, and her smooth face was lined with worry.

"Perhaps I'll just do the unification here," Bulan said. "We can't go on like this for days, waiting for help."

"I can try to distract him again." Bagyo floated beside Bulan. Their plan of dressing a fallen tree branch with Bulan's clothes had failed. Kidlat had been distracted, but only for a few moments, not long enough for them to get into the lake of life.

"No," Bulan said. "What about the hidden tree? Is it strong enough to pull a demigod's soul?"

"No, but..." Bugna tilted her head. "It can pull your mortal soul."

I could hide there, Bulan thought. But then Kidlat

could steal her mortal body and catch her soul when she returned. He needed her mortal body to catch her demigod's soul, and her body couldn't stay alive without a soul.

"He's coming." Bugna raised a hand and transported them to a place she'd never seen before. Bugna leaned against a tree, looking like she was about to pass out.

Bulan searched for something to eat. They hadn't eaten since the previous night, and she was starving. None of the trees around seemed to bear fruit. They were on top of a mountain, and when she looked down, she thought she saw the great river.

"We're near the town. Or maybe not. This river looks different." She stumbled upon a white stone. She jumped back as she got a better view of the sculpture of a man. "This is a graveyard."

"Lin-ay! What are you doing here? I thought you were in the lake of life." Una was running toward them with Dasig behind.

"Kidlat is coming for us. You must leave, or Kidlat will suspect you," Bugna said.

"We can't," Una replied. "I'm here to claim my ancestor's power."

"That's not important right now, Una. Kidlat wouldn't hesitate to kill you," Bulan said.

"Linog. I need Linog to help you," Una said as Linog appeared beside her with a mischievous grin.

"No wonder."

Since Bulan had started seeing her own past, she'd

thought Una was familiar but never really gave it a thought until right then. "We're leaving, then. We can't risk you getting found here."

"Wait! Don't tell me you'll keep flying until Kidlat catches up to you," Una said. "You need a concealer. Wait... Datu Habagat told me he gave you half of his concealer."

"It's not enough to hide Bagyo's power. We need more, bigger, like the prison cell in the Bolo Warrior Barangay, but Kidlat knew all the rooms with concealers. Once we disappear from his senses, he'll check those first." Bulan counted on her fingers the rooms she knew—four places so far, one in the Bolo Warrior Barangay, one in Datu Habagat's house, another under Mariit Inn, and the last in Dungog's underground.

"There's one he doesn't know," Una said, crossing her arms and grinning proudly.

"Where?" Bugna asked.

"Tanda's house. He has an underground."

"Tanda? I still don't know if I could fully trust that man."

"He helped us two times without expecting anything in return," Bulan said. "I trust him."

"But if Kidlat finds us, many lives will be lost. There are too many houses crammed together in town," Bugna argued.

"It's the best choice you have, old shaman. Kidlat wouldn't think you'll hide in his territory. Besides, most people around his house are dead anyway... or possessed by the souls. And... you need some rest. You look ugly without sleep." Una took some smoked meat from her bag, teasing Bulan and Bugna as she took a bite. "Tanda has plenty of food too."

"The town is big. Where's his house?" Bugna asked, suddenly sounding eager. "Describe the surroundings in detail."

"It's near the river," Una said after swallowing. "If you cross the river from Lin-ay's old house, there's a road straight from the river. You count three roads to the north and take that. And maybe... hmmm. Let's see. Ten, eleven... I'm not sure how many stone houses from the river."

"It's not enough," Bugna said. "Describe his house. Any particular sound or smell."

"Oh!" Una said, her face brightening with realization. "He has cocks. Gamecocks. Many of them. You can hear them crowing all the time. And they smell too. He has a lot of those small little roofs behind his house for the roosters' shelter. I don't think anyone else has roosters on the same street."

"Thank you." Bugna bowed.

Una's eyes widened in surprise, and even Bulan was surprised at the shaman's politeness.

"And be careful," Bugna continued. "Once you take the power out of the earthen jar, Kidlat will sense it."

"Don't trust Linog too much," Bulan added. "I wouldn't be surprised if she wanted you dead. Bagyo almost killed me when I searched for his power."

"Come on, now." Linog raised an eyebrow. "She's

my descendant. Why would I want her dead? She'll be my anchor here in the world of the living."

"You should ask Bagyo." Bulan side-eyed Bagyo.

"Enough!" Bugna massaged her temples. "We'll get going. If Kidlat finds you here, make an excuse or something. I'm counting on you, Una."

In a blink, Bulan was hearing surprised roosters in a chorus of alarm. They'd landed in the middle of the small roofs Una had described.

"How did you find this place?" Bulan asked.

"By imagining it," Bugna answered. She massaged her temples again as they headed toward the kitchen door. "You must have noticed we've been traveling to the same places. That's because I can't go to a place I don't know."

Bulan opened the kitchen door and jumped as she stared back at Una. "Wh-what are you doing here?" *She couldn't have flown that fast.*

"Una told me you'd be here." Putot appeared behind Una. "Hurry. The underground's ready." Her short legs were almost invisible as she led them inside.

Bulan and Bugna followed without question, but Bulan couldn't help looking back at Una, whose face changed into that of Tanda's. The stairs were steeper and smaller than that of the Mariit Inn. Anting-anting lights were hung to the sides. Tanda pulled a slab of stone back to cover the opening behind them. People unknown to Bulan bowed as she reached the bottom of the stairs.

"How did you talk to Una?" she asked Putot.

"Through a tracker. I'm injecting trackers into all shamans who are on our side," Putot said. She transformed into a snake in a heartbeat.

"How can this be?" Tanda paced around the circle of shamans sitting cross-legged on the floor. "It means Kidlat is near. We were hoping to have a few more days to gather all those who can help us. Habagat and a few powerful shamans are on their way to the lake of life, but they're not enough. Kidlat could kill us before we could even leave. If he goes back to the inn, he would know I replaced the prisoners with banana stems."

"Banana stems?" Bulan asked.

"Yes. They'll eventually die in a few days and turn back into stems, but Kidlat could sense the anting-antings. He has a sharp sense. He would figure out they're not real people."

"Then we have to hurry," Bugna said. "I suspect you know how to absorb magic into the body."

Tanda didn't hesitate. He rushed to a cabinet against a wall and took out some bottles. "It'll hurt. May the good spirits guide us. It could kill her if her body rejects it."

"What are you doing?" Bagyo asked in a dangerous low tone. "My power is for my descendants."

"Bagyo." Bugna bowed. When she straightened, she winced as if trying to fight against Datu Habagat, who was trying to control her speech. When she spoke again, the voice was Datu Habagat's. "Please let Bulan use your power. We'll figure out how to transfer it later after we defeat Kidlat."

"Pathetic." Bagyo sneered. "You're my descendant? Don't you know that if Bulan becomes too powerful, the earth could become her playground? Other gods would crush this place out of jealousy."

"I will not hold on to power!" Bulan shouted angrily. The world was in danger, yet all Bagyo could think about was who was more powerful.

"I trust Lin-ay," Datu Habagat said. "I trust she will save Makanas because Makanas is Bakunawa. Please" —Datu Habagat bowed—"let Bulan borrow your power. My son needs her."

"But aren't you forgetting something?" Bagyo huffed. "This room is lined with a concealer. Your magic won't work."

Tanda dropped his bamboo container and looked at Putot. "Right. I forgot about that. But why have your trackers worked?"

"She was partly an afterlife being. Her tracker is of the afterlife's power, and so is the concealer," Bugna said, her gaze returning to her usual calm demeanor, indicating Datu Habagat had retreated. "But absorbing power is still a new magic and hasn't been tested against concealers."

Tanda scratched his chin. "We can do the ceremony separately. It's only needed to strengthen her body for the magic. We'll leave the bone here underground and insert it into her body after the ceremony."

"Fool! She needs to stay in the circle," Bugna said.

"The circle doesn't need to be on the ground," Tanda

argued. "I've tried on the second floor, and it worked just fine. If we fail, we'll lose nothing."

"Except time, which we don't have." Bugna crossed her arms. "And you should know better not to mess with ceremonies."

"We'll run out of time if we keep on hesitating," Tanda said, his face turning red. "You're no better a shaman than I am. You criticized Kidlat for being stubborn, but you are worse than him."

"Stop!" Bulan stepped between them. "We can try that or wait until Una retrieves Linog's power and travel to the lake of life together. She and I have a higher chance of defeating Kidlat even if we don't absorb the powers. But..." She inhaled deeply to calm herself, not wanting to offend Bugna. "I think we must at least try. Based on my experience with retrieving Bagyo's power, it'll take at least a day or two for Una to reach it, even with her anting-antings."

Tanda and Bugna stared at each other. Tension rose in the air as two shamans who'd both lived on earth for thousands of years measured each other. Bulan was afraid they would argue again, but Bugna nodded.

Bulan unbuttoned her pocket. "I trust you to keep this while they do the ceremony outside," she said, holding out Bagyo's bone.

"Of course, goddess." Putot bowed her head low and held out two hands.

"Just call me Bulan." She gently put the bone into Putot's hands and followed Tanda and Bugna upstairs.

Tanda led them to a room on the second floor, where

he spread a white blanket on the floor and asked Bulan to lie down. It smelled like the man hadn't washed it for moons, but Bulan didn't complain and breathed through her mouth.

Bugna turned away and fanned her nose. "Ugh. Hurry and draw." She opened the window.

"Have you gone insane? People will recognize your face," Tanda said in a hushed voice.

"No, they won't," Bugna said with confidence and stuck her head outside.

Tanda poured black powder around Bulan in a circle. Then he made a line outward connecting Bulan's belly button to the circle. "Don't move." He did the same with her feet, hands, and head, connecting them with the circle. Then he fetched four lamps and set them just outside the circle. "It's ready. Close the window."

"Bulan," Bugna said in a controlled voice. "You'll travel beyond the world of the living. It's like your experience in the hidden tree except this world will be created by you. Your mind will open up to your deepest fears. You have to fight what needs to be fought and accept things you can't change."

"How do I get back?" Bulan asked, reminded of how the hidden tree had tricked her. She wasn't afraid of fighting her fears. Bakunawa was already dead, which was her worst fear. She couldn't think of anything worse than that.

"We can hear you. You only have to say the words. But if Kidlat appears before we finish, find the door.

You must memorize what it looks like before opening it for the first time."

Bulan's heart drummed. "What happens if I summon my spirit?"

"We have no idea," Tanda answered. "Best not to do it. You can do that later, when the world is at peace and you have time to explore. Ready?"

Bulan nodded even though she wasn't. Tanda lit a small piece of wood and brought it down to the black powder comprising the circle. Bulan's first thought was that the blanket would catch fire, but the fire only traveled along the powder. The fire touched her skin but didn't burn.

"Hum with us, Bulan." Tanda started humming in a low, almost inaudible voice.

Bugna joined him. When Bulan hummed subconsciously, a sudden surge of energy exploded in her head. It felt like the jolt she got just when she was about to fall asleep and have nightmares, but it was stronger that time. She couldn't see anything in the dark, but she had the sensation of falling.

"This isn't your place, Bulan."

Bulan turned and saw Dilim sucking the light out of the world of the living. She realized they weren't lights but the souls of the living. People were dropping to the ground in great numbers like rain. Bulan flew to the lake of life because Bathala needed to know, but the lake of life was barren. The land once full of colorful liquid was just a hollow on earth. The soil was cracked as if it hadn't had rain for years. Only the trunk remained of the tree in the middle. She screamed for Bathala but heard no answer. She couldn't ascend.

"Bakunawa!" she called.

The serpent appeared on the horizon, flying elegantly but quickly. Bulan met Bakunawa, caressed his face, and flew alongside him. Dilim fled upon seeing them, but he had nowhere to go. Bakunawa was more powerful than he, even in the afterlife. She wondered why that was so, when Dilim was the god of the world of the dead, but she had no time to think. Bakunawa coiled around Dilim until he turned to ashes.

"Bakunawa, let's return to the lake of life," Bulan said. "We must find a way to rebuild it."

Bakunawa turned into a man and held her hand. "First, you must wake up."

Bulan's eyes flew open. Bugna and Tanda were still humming. Bulan was eager to see her thread of life but remembered she couldn't summon her spirit. Her eyes closed involuntarily as she felt another jolt like the one she'd experienced earlier. When she opened her eyes again, in a world she knew was made of dreams, she almost wept. She saw no sign of life. Structures had been reclaimed by nature. The buildings were unfamiliar, like they had been erected hundreds or perhaps thousands of years after her lifetime as Lin-ay. She knew she was dreaming or, rather, seeing what was inside her mind, but it felt very real. She touched a stone and felt its coldness. She flew, hoping to find anything that would tell her humanity had survived, but failed.

"In the end, humankind will fail." *What's the use of fighting? Perhaps I should just stay still and watch everything unfold like my father, if he is even watching.* Perhaps Bathala had forgotten about the earth. Maybe he created something new, something that would display his power as the supreme ruler. She had no desire to ascend to the gods' realm either. Fighting about power was tiring. Or perhaps Bathala knew humanity would eventually end, and he was trying to spare her that pain by obliterating life on earth earlier. She sat on a rock to empty her mind of all those worries. Someone said her name, but she didn't see anyone. The voice was frantic and persistent.

"Wake up!" a woman said.

Bulan looked up at the dark sky as she thought the voice was coming from above. But it couldn't have been a god. People looked up at the sky when they called for help, thinking gods were physically above them because when gods appeared, they flew down. They didn't know that the gods' realm was something not located anywhere in relation to the human concept of direction.

"Wake up!" a man shouted. That voice was louder.

Bulan's eyelids felt heavy. She let them close. When she opened her eyes, she was back at Tanda's house.

"How long was I out?" she asked.

"Not even an hour, but your breathing is shallow, and you muttered disturbing words." Tanda shared a look with Bugna. "Bulan, your body is ready. Why didn't you return?"

Bulan couldn't bear to tell them what she'd seen. She felt like walking away to avoid their faces.

Bugna held her down. "The ceremony isn't over. Your body is ready. Now, it's time to absorb the magic."

Tanda held up a small bottle. "This isn't magic. It'll dull the pain but will not eliminate it completely. You must endure the pain. I will create an incision large enough for the bone's entry."

"What if I pass out?" Bulan asked.

"It's absolutely fine. This concoction might actually cause you to sleep. Shamans are healers. You know that. We've trained to heal without magic. We know when to pull the bone out if your body refuses to accept the power."

"Hold me down so I won't move on instinct."

"I'll use magic to suppress the pain while I cut," Tanda said as he tilted the bottle and let the liquid flow into Bulan's mouth. "Close your eyes. You don't want to see me cutting."

"I've been in deadly battles," Bulan said. "This doesn't faze me at all." She stared at the ceiling as she heard Tanda unsheathe his knife. After that, she didn't feel a thing. Her eyes felt heavy. The last thing she was aware of was Tanda and Bugna carrying her on the blanket into the underground.

18

UNA

Una couldn't sense anting-antings, but she could certainly sense Kidlat's rage as he knocked trees out of his way.

"You two are my best warriors. You should have risked your lives to stop them." Kidlat gritted his teeth.

"I'm sorry, Head Warrior. They disappeared before we could even get near them. We searched but didn't find them," Una said, head bowed.

"And why are you here?" Kidlat faced Una. "You two have different missions."

Una was afraid to look at Dasig. He wasn't a good liar, so she decided to speak first. "I've searched almost everywhere for Amihan but didn't find them. I thought of coming here because Amihan visited here before, when I was young. She knew my family... but as you can see, the barangay is gone. And he"—she tilted her head toward Dasig—"thought Lin-ay would want to find her mother."

Kidlat's nostrils flared. "I need the two of you to stay right here. I don't care if it's weeks or moons. You stay here and stop them as soon as they appear. I'm sure they will come this way again."

"Yes, Head Warrior," Una said as Dasig bowed in acknowledgement. "That was close!" Una sighed as Kidlat flew away.

"Be quiet," Dasig growled.

"He's gone. I should call Li—"

"No." Dasig shot her a warning look. "He could return to check. He doesn't trust anyone."

"Come on. He has better things to do."

But Dasig was right. Kidlat appeared out of nowhere just as Una was about to call Linog for direction.

"I need one of you to return to the inn." Kidlat said in a calm voice, erasing his outburst earlier in their minds. "The other should stay here on guard. Dungog's shaman will plant a tracker on you to make it easy for me to talk to you."

"He agreed to help you?" Una couldn't help but ask.

She wondered what would happen if the shaman learned they already had trackers. Kidlat would torture them to confess. Perhaps he knew they were helping Lin-ay. She wanted to volunteer and make up some story about why she couldn't receive the tracker, but she couldn't give up on her mission to get Linog's power.

"I'll get the tracker first," Dasig said in an unwavering voice that surprised Una.

"You can't…" Una said, holding his hand.

"I don't have weak warriors," Kidlat approached them until his face was but a few inches away. "You must sacrifice for the greater good, understand?"

Una couldn't help but nod.

"Fine." Kidlat turned. "I don't think they'll be back here soon. I bet they'll go somewhere else first. Regardless, you must guard this place, Warrior Una."

"Understood, Head Warrior."

"And you also need a tracker later. Just to make sure you're safe from the souls." Then Kidlat flew away, snapping branches from the trees he passed by.

"I'm afraid you must do this on your own from now on." Dasig squeezed her hand.

"How can you pretend? You're not a good liar. Perhaps you can fetch Linog's power. I can lie, even to myself. I'll get injected instead."

"No. You deserve to get the power yourself. I'll make this work."

"Make an excuse. Or wait for at least a week to get it done. Kidlat can't get back here in a day or two."

"I'll try to stall it, but the longer it takes, the more suspicious he'll be. We can't have him suspecting a rebellion."

Una knew Dasig was right. "Pass by Tanda's house. Maybe he can help. Maybe he can alter your memory or something. I don't know… but you must not receive the tracker. Kidlat will kill you."

"I need to see Putot anyway." Dasig kissed her on the forehead. "Be careful."

After Dasig left, Una summoned Linog and asked him to help locate his tomb. Dasig wouldn't be back for at least two days, so she needed to make use of the time when Kidlat couldn't see her.

Linog told Una to dig up his grave. She cut down a small tree, sharpened it, and dug. Even with her anting-antings giving her strength, the work was slow, and she wished she had at least a shovel. When the edge of the hole reached her chest, she finally found a rock that Linog had told her to seek. As expected, the grave was empty.

As Linog had instructed, she cleaned the rock and pushed the white stone beside it. The earth before her collapsed, forming a dark tunnel. Flying wasn't an option, for the tunnel was so small that her head touched the ceiling. She had to crouch and touch the sides with her hands to guide herself.

"Why didn't you tell me to bring a lamp?" Una asked.

"I forgot. You know, we didn't need lamps in the afterlife," Linog said. "Stop! If I remember correctly, my first trap is here. Put one foot forward just firmly enough for the land to think you're standing on it."

"I can't see anything! What if I step too far?" Una then lowered her voice because Linog was a demigod. She should show some respect, at least. "Sorry."

"Put a foot forward." Linog paused, waiting for Una to move. "More," she said as Una moved. "A little bit more. Dear spirits, Una. You can fly. Why are you so afraid of falling?"

Una wanted to roll her eyes. "I thought a rock would crush me. Or perhaps arrows would hit me." Una stepped forward and flew as the ground collapsed underneath her. "You should learn more tricks than creating holes. It's getting predictable."

"Ha! I didn't know I had an all-knowing descendant. Find my bones by yourself."

"No!" Una looked around but saw nothing but darkness. "I was just kidding. I'm deeply sorry, goddess of earthquake."

Linog didn't answer. Una knew what body part held Linog's power, but the goddess hadn't revealed all the traps to her. If she failed, Makanas would die, as well as Lin-ay, Dasig, herself, and probably many more. "Me and my smart mouth," she muttered.

She flew slowly. Quite soon, the tunnel widened, with anting-anting lights to guide her way.

Una passed three more challenges without getting hurt. Linog didn't show up, but Una grew more confident with her progress. She didn't know how long she'd been underground, but based on how hungry she was, the afternoon must have come already. She stopped for a quick meal then resumed her journey. She plucked one anting-anting light from the wall and thought herself lucky that she didn't need to go back and make a torch. The passage turned dark and narrow, making flight impossible again. It reminded her of the entrance to Linog's grave. The journey grew dull as no new traps appeared for her to solve.

Then Una screamed as the ground shook and

collapsed. She remembered how to fly just before she hit the ground. She breathed deeply to calm her heart. *Linog really needs to come up with a different strategy.* She laughed, thinking Linog was indeed an easygoing demigod, until she encountered the next challenge, which was exactly the same as the second since she'd entered. She tried to tell herself that was impossible, but then she reached the brighter part of the underground with anting-anting lights and confirmed that one of them was missing. She stopped, not knowing what to do. She hadn't noticed any curve that indicated she was going in circles, yet she knew better than to move forward and take the same route.

"Linog, please answer my prayer. I need your help."

She felt revulsion at hearing her own words, for she hated begging and praying. Gods hadn't answered her even once in her whole life, but that might have been because she didn't like calling them. Her words were considered rude by shamans, and she'd never felt that memorizing shamans' words would help.

"Please," she added, making her voice smaller.

"Don't trust Linog too much." Lin-ay's words echoed in her head. She didn't understand why Linog couldn't simply hand her the power. She was a descendant. If Lin-ay had retrieved Bagyo's power without anting-antings, Una could surely do it.

"Right," she said. "I forgot I could talk to Putot. Putot? Can you hear me?"

"Yes," Putot said in her small voice.

"Can you talk to Bugna?"

"Yes, she's here." Putot paused then said, "It's Una."

"Can you ask her how to summon Linog by force? She disappeared on me and won't answer."

"She said it's not possible because she's not your companion yet."

"Ugh. Damn it. Well, thank you anyway. Tell her it might take me longer. I'm going in circles. Perhaps Lin-ay can give me some tips from Bulan's memories of Linog."

"I'm sorry," Putot said in a thin, worried voice. "Bulan is unconscious. Her body is fighting Bagyo's power. We still don't know when she's going to wake up."

"Unconscious?" Una realized that if Lin-ay died, Makanas, her closest friend aside from Dasig would also die. "If she dies, I'm going to behead those two shamans myself.

"She'll be fine," Putot said though she didn't sound sure.

Una told Putot about Dasig and asked her to tell Tanda to help him.

Then she looked around the anting-anting lights because that was the last place she'd been before circling back to the starting point. Only one path existed, so the problem wasn't even choosing the right one. The ceiling was made of jagged black rocks, and beneath her feet was the soft soil. Her head was pounding from lack of sleep.

"I'm too impatient for this kind of shit," she heard herself saying.

Then she sighed. She really needed to fix her habit of saying her thoughts aloud. That had brought her trouble countless times. She put the anting-anting light back on the wall to free her hand and noticed the rocks shift. It was so subtle that if she hadn't been looking in the direction of the dark path ahead, she wouldn't have noticed. *Ah. That trickster Linog. I better not touch anything again.*

Una continued her journey, resting only for quick meals. She was too stubborn to beg Linog's help, and her many anting-antings were strong enough to help her fight the creatures Linog had created to stop anyone from getting her power. The only thing bothering Una was drowsiness and impatience due to lack of sleep. Even with the anting-anting that replenished her energy, her eyes felt heavy, and she longed to lie down.

Just after she ate the last bit of her two-day rations of smoked meat, Una finally saw the earthen jar Linog had described. The jar was old and decorated with green moss, but beneath it was a hat-shaped golden stone supporting its weight. She knew better than to rush up and touch it. She looked around, noting the square room. No other path existed aside from the one she was following. The walls were completely black, reminding her of the concealer in Tanda's underground. Then she realized something. She couldn't sense her anting-antings. She retreated as soon as the ground moved, but she was too late as the door closed with a loud bang.

Her heart racing, she stabbed the wall, but it wasn't made of soil like the others but of cold, hard black stone. Her eyes involuntarily looked up, and as expected, the ceiling was made of the same black concealer with jagged edges. Lin-ay was right. The gods must have been selfish, and Linog wanted her dead just to keep her power away. She put a hand against her forehead, trying to calm herself. Her head spun. *I'm feeling sick*, she thought, but when she tried to focus, she realized she was dizzy because the room was actually spinning. She stepped closer to the wall, but the gap between it and the floor was so narrow that the edge of her blade wouldn't even fit.

Confusion took over as the spot on the wall where she tried to stab moved down. No, it didn't move down. The floor itself was moving up. It was going to crush her. *How can I fight the soil itself?* She had expected demons, gigantic animals, or some crazy, powerful human guardian.

Am I going to die before we can even try to help Makanas? She crouched as a protruding rock touched her head. An idea came to her. Surely, Linog didn't want his bones crushed. She looked up again, that time concentrating on the ceiling directly above the earthen jar. Linog had tried to trick her by making her think she shouldn't touch anything before, when she had to return the anting-anting light.

With slow, steady steps, Una approached the jar, and with every step, the ceiling sank more quickly. She rolled as fast as she could and hugged the earthen jar, not to protect it but to protect her own body. The rocks slammed against each other in a loud crash around her.

The small space left was just barely enough for the earthen jar and her body. She couldn't even lift her head up. She tightened her grip, but without her anting-anting, the jar didn't even crack. She must have been foolish to think it would be fragile like the others.

She took a ragged breath. *This must be how it feels to be buried alive.* "Damn you, Linog. You better make sure I don't get out of here alive." *If I have the strength to be angry, I better do something before I die of suffocation.* Inch by inch, she moved a hand up toward the mouth of the jar. She gritted her teeth as she forced her fingers into a tighter space between the wall and the jar. Warm blood trickled down her wrist, and she thought she might faint. She almost cried as her hand reached the mouth of the jar.

In the dark, she rummaged through the bones, still intact even after thousands of years. Strength and power hit her with a jolt as her hand found Linog's big toe. Then the rocks moved at her command, lifting her upward until she broke the surface. All her anting-anting powers came back. She felt like she was reborn as a new person as every scratch on her body healed.

"You are indeed worthy, my brave descendant." Linog floated over and tried to touch Una's head in a blessing.

"I don't need you anymore." Una sneered. "You can just hide in the afterlife, for all I care." She flew past Linog, looking for anything familiar that could indicate her location. From the top of a mountain, she saw the balete tree on another mountain ahead. She hadn't traveled far.

"Putot, can you hear me? Putot?"

"U-una," Putot seemed hesitant to talk to her.

"I have Linog's power. Tell Bugna to come get me and bring me to the lake of life."

"The thing is... they left yesterday to find you. If they're not there, they must be headed to the lake of life now."

"They should've waited for me!"

Putot kept silent for a long time. "We couldn't because... Maybe we should talk about this in person. I think we're near your barangay."

"Tell me now." Una's heart drummed. She thought she knew what had happened, but her heart wasn't ready.

"Kidlat knows our plan."

"Did Dasig tell him?"

"No. Some of the shamans on our side were tortured after they refused to get injected by Dungog's shaman."

"And Dasig?"

"He... he passed away yesterday."

Una sank to her knees. Her scream echoed throughout the mountains. The rocks rolled. The ground shook.

"Una! That power is for saving people, not destroying." Linog floated in front of her with pleading eyes.

"If you hadn't wasted my time, Dasig wouldn't have died, you pompous bitch!"

Birds shrieked and fled as an entire mountain collapsed.

Linog shrank back. "Humans are fragile. If I'd just handed you the power without a test, it could've fallen into evil hands."

"Fragile? I curse you. May Dilim hold you tight, and you'll never see the land of the living again."

"No!" Linog screamed. "You need me as your companion. You don't know how to handle the power."

Una might have never seen the gate to the underworld, but she knew the two worlds collided at that moment. Lightning without sound flashed in the sky. Then the world turned dark, and an invisible force pulled Linog back until she disappeared. When that brief moment passed, the earthquake stopped, and Una saw the destruction she had caused. Three mountains were flattened as though a giant had stepped on them, but not much else was disturbed.

Una wanted to see if she could heal the land, to make the mountains stand as they were before. *Heal? All of this happened because we wanted to save Makanas.* Perhaps they could also save Dasig by having Iyay perform a returning ceremony. If Dasig had died the day before, his soul was still in the world of the living.

"Putot? Putot!" she screamed, demanding immediate attention.

"Una!"

Una turned because the voice wasn't in her head. Putot was riding her white cat and leading a group of flying shamans, about a hundred. Una met them, flying faster than she ever had. Linog's power had amplified every anting-antings she had.

"We have to get to Dasig," Una said. "Right now, Iyay!"

Iyay was sitting behind Putot. "We can't, child," She shook her head slowly, as if she had read Una's mind. She tapped Putot's shoulder so that Putot would urge her cat to land. "I would've if I could've, but he was beheaded, and when we located him, we were too late to heal him. Without a body, the soul can't return."

"He can't die like that! He needs to die in battle. To prove his honor." Una landed, weak despite having a demigod's power at her disposal.

"He did die honorably. He battled with Kidlat's warriors in the inn despite being tortured by Kidlat." Iyay stepped down from the cat and hugged Una tightly.

Una bawled like a child, just as she did when Iyay had held her when she was young.

"Kidlat is my son," Iyay said, "but he needs to be punished. You have to brace yourself to face him. If he isn't stopped, the world itself will die."

Iyay was right. After Una punished Kidlat, she could die peacefully. She would never die before his death.

She pushed Iyay's hands away gently. "I can fly faster, but like Bugna, I can only bring a limited number of people."

"Bulan classified us based on the strength of our

anting-antings. You must bring me and Head Guard Uwak," Putot said.

"We'll catch up with you. Help Bulan get into the lake of life. That is all we need," Iyay said.

Una held the hands of Head Guard Uwak and Putot, who passed on the directions to the lake of life.

As the cool wind touched Una's face, her mind cleared. "I haven't seen Tanda."

"He's hunting Kidlat's shaman," Head Guard Uwak said. "Their communication needed to be cut off."

That move was late, Una thought. If they'd only known the shaman was siding with Kidlat, they could've eliminated him and prevented Dasig's death.

"I'm sorry that you don't even get to mourn." Head Guard Uwak squeezed Una's hand tightly.

Una blinked away her tears. She hated crying in front of others, but Head Guard Uwak had known her since she was a child and, like Iyay, had seen her in her weakest moments. "Ending Kidlat is more than enough to erase my grief. After this is over, I will follow him to the afterlife."

"You must trust the gods' will," Putot said. "It is said that the gods listen to those with great deeds. Perhaps they can help Dasig be reborn faster."

Una chuckled. She couldn't imagine meeting a newborn Dasig. "I don't think the gods care about us one bit. We're but pawns to fuel their greed."

"Dear spirits, how can you say that? What if they hear you?"

"If they do, they should've cut down the evil people and sent them straight to the afterlife."

"Well, that's not how it works."

"They can surely make it that way." Una found herself smiling despite her grief. If the gods could indeed bring Dasig back to life, she would have the strength to live after her revenge. She considered whom she could call for help. She would ask Lin-ay. Bulan would surely remember who among the gods would pity Una.

They continued flying for days above lands and endless seas that Una hadn't seen before. In the midst of all the chaos, Una wished she had the chance to fly with Dasig, not for a competition, not for a mission, but just because they wanted to.

"Stop!" Putot gripped Una's hand tighter.

Una didn't have time to ask what was wrong as ten shamans surrounded them. They moved so quickly that Una hadn't seen them coming. The shamans chanted, and light traveled through their joined hands.

Una let go of Habagat and Putot. The head guard caught Putot as the shaman dropped. The shamans didn't care about the two of them, concentrating only on Una. News must have reached them that she'd gained the power of a demigod. She tried to rise, but streaks of light hit her and made movement impossible. However, she could still feel her anting-antings and Linog's power.

Putot transformed into a snake, and the gigantic snake bashed her head against the circle of shamans, breaking their formation. That was all Una needed. In deep concentration, she called forth rocks from the earth, and they rose at her command, higher and higher. The shamans had no chance to flee. Rocks rained on them and buried them deep in the ground.

Una shook her head, unable to believe she'd almost been defeated by ten mere shamans when she had Linog's power. The rocks and soil listened to her and responded to her emotions, but the power still felt foreign. Perhaps she'd been wrong to banish Linog. In fact, she hadn't known that banishing a companion back to the underworld was possible.

"We're a good team!" Una said to Putot as Head Guard Uwak rose and carried the girl back to Una. She held their hands again and flew faster.

"Makanas is a better warrior," Putot said. "I haven't fought any battles. I don't have a warrior's impulses. Anyway, I asked you to stop because Habagat told me there are stronger shamans ahead. The ones we just fought are the last and the least powerful."

"Then why didn't Lin-ay just kill them?"

"Because they were fighting the stronger shamans. Bugna decided to keep Kidlat's forces scattered. If they were together, it'd be harder to fight and easier for Kidlat to catch Bulan. Wait… Tanda's speaking to me."

"What did he say?"

"They caught Kidlat's shaman."

19

THE CHANTER

"Now. We should attack now that we have struck the first blow." Datu Habagat wiped at the blood on his face, and it spread even wider, making him look like a savage animal that had just finished his prey. "How far are we?"

"I can transport us there in one go," Bugna answered.

"No," Bulan said. "Have you forgotten that Bagyo belongs to the lower pantheon? I need Una. We must wait." They'd had a solid plan days before, which was shattered when Kidlat started killing warriors and shamans on their side. She prayed Putot would stay safe so that they could talk to each other as they attack.

"Don't belittle me." Bagyo appeared, but filmy, as if he was just a trick of the eye.

Bulan ignored him. "Kidlat didn't know that his second batch of shamans are now dead. We must go back, eliminate the second-to-last shamans, and let Una go first to distract Kidlat."

"But if Kidlat's strongest shamans get there first, it'd be impossible for us to fight them. We must kill them first."

"They must be close to the lake of life now," Bulan said. "Bakunawa belongs to the higher pantheon. Kidlat might not have the power to transport like Bugna, but he'll get to us in no time. We'll be trapped before we even get close to the lake of life."

Bulan and Habagat argued on, each giving solid reasons. They were transported before they even knew it.

Bulan stared into Bugna's impassive eyes and said, "Let's hope this is the right choice."

"Better than arguing and doing nothing," Bugna answered.

The shamans tried to flee when they saw Bulan, but they were slow. Bulan made sure no one escaped. She knew Kidlat was anxious for news since he couldn't communicate with his shamans anymore.

"It's time you have this." Bulan untied the bakunawa blade from her waist and handed it to Datu Habagat. She was thankful that Tanda had the required anting-antings that had helped Bugna fix the two swords. While Bulan was unconscious and her body struggled to absorb Bagyo's powers, Bugna worked on the blades tirelessly. Tanda and Bugna had hoped the blades would give Bulan the advantage against Kidlat. When Bulan's body successfully absorbed Bagyo's power, they had decided to give one of the blades to Tanda to help him battle against Kidlat's shamans remaining in town.

Datu bowed and accepted the blade with two hands. "If this is to be my last battle, I will face Dilim bravely. It is a great honor to fight alongside you, Bulan."

"You must not die before Bakunawa wakes up. You caused her mortal mother's death. Pay for it in his own terms."

Datu Habagat tilted his head. "It is true that I kidnapped his mother and that I forced her to have my child, but I did not kill her."

"That doesn't matter now—"

"Where is that bastard?"

Bulan turned to see Una holding Putot's and Head Guard Uwak's hands. Rage was boiling in her eyes. Bulan was certain she could've seen Una swirling with power, if she'd had her own spirit right then. Even with her human eyes, she could sense something different about the way Una was wielding her power. She was dangerous.

"We're still far from the lake of life," Bugna answered. "But we'll give him to you if you promise to stay level-headed. Don't get yourself killed before we take Bakunawa out."

"You don't have to worry about that."

Bulan was glad Una wasn't dwelling on her sorrow. She stayed behind as Bugna transported Una and Datu Habagat first. In a matter of a few breaths, Bugna was back. The shaman then took her hand, and in a blink, the lake of life came into full view.

Bulan flew down to hide in the leaves of a balete tree. Kidlat wouldn't be able to detect her power, but his vision was enhanced by Bakunawa's power, and about ten shamans were surrounding the lake of life. Kidlat was nowhere in sight. Bulan was too anxious to stay still, and her human emotions were trying to override her reason.

"As we planned, stay hidden until everyone is in place." Bugna disappeared to get more shamans in position. She was powerful and fast, but she couldn't carry many powerful people in one go.

Kidlat came into view, and Bulan had to grip the balete tree tight to stop herself from flying to the lake of life to strike him. She knew he'd sensed Datu Habagat above. "Una, please stay low," she mumbled to herself.

Una's power lay in the earth, and if she flew high to help Datu Habagat, she couldn't use her power to its full potential. Bulan hoped Una had at least a clue about how to use Linog's power.

An immense blast of air blew the clouds away, exposing the descending Datu Habagat. As he and Kidlat clashed, their swords produced streaks of lightning.

Bulan took a deep breath. *One, two, three. Dear spirits, grant me patience.* Her human side was praying. For a moment, she forgot she was a goddess, and in that moment, she hoped the gods would hear her and take action.

The mountain to the east exploded, the sound louder than anything she'd ever heard. Not even Linog, the god who shook the earth, had expressed such rage. The shamans gathered, shocked by such power. As the earth beneath their feet opened, they flew, as though afraid the soil would swallow them. Kidlat gave one last swing and flew toward the east as Una slowly revealed herself.

Hurry, Bugna, hurry. Bulan clasped her hands in a prayer.

Datu Habagat faced the ten shamans alone, clearly at a disadvantage despite his unmatched fighting skills. Each time he tried to slice one, another would attack him from behind. He rose, taking advantage of the darkening sky. Bulan hoped none of the shamans could detect anting-antings.

Kidlat approached Una calmly. Every rock Una hurled shattered before it could touch him. She was like fire, and he, water, dousing Una's fury. Earth rose around Una, as if the earth itself was alive. It turned into the shape of a gigantic man and smashed Kidlat. Kidlat slashed the soil man. It toppled but regained its form. It reminded Bulan of the sandman she'd fought when she searched for Bagyo's power. It was an incredible display of power, considering that Una had only had the power for a day. *How did she learn to do that trick?*

Despite Una's tricks, Kidlat was stronger. The longer the fight took, the weaker Una became. Bulan desperately wanted to approach the lake of life, but Kidlat was too close, and the ten shamans still fought against Datu Habagat directly above the lake of life.

Bugna, where are you? She should've been back already. Bulan couldn't talk to Putot because her body had refused the tracker. Kidlat slashed the soil man's ankles, and it toppled, failing to form again. Kidlat landed on the ground and walked slowly toward Una, the bakunawa blade brightening in his hand. *Una is going to die.*

Bulan inhaled her spirit back into her body. She summoned thunder, rain, and wind at the same time. Kidlat was swept off his feet, causing his strike to miss. Una was shouting at Bulan to go away, but it was too late for that.

"Bigger. Stronger. I need something powerful."

"A tornado," Bagyo answered.

He angled his body directly in front of her, guiding her movements until a tornado that reached the sky was wreaking havoc on the earth. Kidlat was fast, but Bulan trapped him inside the violent vortex of air.

Bulan seized that distraction and flew toward the lake of life. But as soon as her concentration was broken, the tornado disappeared. Bulan gasped as a blade pierced through her stomach. The lake of life was mere feet away. *I can't die now.*

Kidlat slashed his own stomach without flinching and took out the snare ball. "The gods will never look down on us ever again." His wound healed in a blink.

A rock flew toward Kidlat, but he simply laughed as he kicked away Una's attempt at distracting him.

Bulan recovered from her momentary shock. Behind Kidlat, Datu Habagat was struggling to reach him, but three shamans were holding him in place with threads of magic.

The stab was a mortal wound. Even gods wouldn't heal quickly from the bakunawa blade. Then memories poured into her like salvation. The blade was a part of her and was designed not to harm her. Kidlat frowned as the blade slowly ejected from her body on its own, leaving Bulan's wound to close. More memories poured in, as if the blade had fed them to her.

"No!" Kidlat screamed and pushed the blade into Bulan's body again.

Bulan gasped. In the corner of her eyes, Una was crawling toward Kidlat, desperately bidding the ground to rise. Bulan waited and stared into Kidlat's cold, dark gaze as he drove the blade deeper.

Now. She grabbed his hand. *Blade, come to me. Return home.* The blade stirred. The cold metal turned warm and soft. Slowly, it shrank smaller and smaller.

Kidlat withdrew his hand, surprise and fear unmistakable in his eyes. But Bulan's grip made sure he could not pull the blade out. She held his hand tightly until the blade turned back into her bone. Bulan felt a part of herself returning. She was almost complete.

Guilt seeped into her. If she had only been able to remember, she could've prevented countless deaths. She took advantage of Kidlat's surprise and grabbed the snare ball in his hand, ripping his flesh as he held onto it. She yanked until his arm separated from his body.

Bulan threw his arm on the ground and stared at the bloody snare ball. She finally had Bakunawa back.

"No!" Kidlat screamed, but his voice was cut off as Bulan's hand circled his throat. "Bu-Bug-Bugna."

Bulan loosened her grip, remembering that Bugna hadn't returned.

"If you kill me now, you will not see Bugna again." Kidlat flashed his teeth despite her hand circling his throat. He angled his body toward his torn arm on the ground. The arm moved as though it was alive and rejoined his body.

Bulan contemplated. Even without the blade, the evil bastard was still powerful. She looked at Datu Habagat, who'd finally broken free from the shamans' snare. She summoned lightning to hit two of them. The last one flew away, but Datu Habagat threw his blade to cut off her head.

"Now, I can think clearly," she said as she focused on Kidlat and realized she'd been choking him harder unconsciously. "Speak." She loosened her grip again.

But Kidlat kept his mouth shut.

"Where is Bugna?"

"Weak," Kidlat spat.

"No, you are weak." Bulan tightened her grip. "You let greed and anger take over your heart."

"Bulan! You're going to kill him." Datu Habagat landed behind Kidlat. "I'll go back and search for Bugna."

"No," Bulan said. "I'd rather you stay here. I bet you'll enjoy him."

Datu Habagat's eyebrows rose, and he smiled as he understood what she meant. "Alive?"

"Yes," Bulan answered. "You know where they are, right?"

Datu Habagat's smile widened. "Hmm. Some are completely absorbed. I can't get them unless I drink his blood, but I see one in his wrist, two in his ankles. My, my, this man has perfected absorbing anting-antings into his body."

Bulan shuddered at the thought and hoped Kidlat would tell them where Bugna was before Datu Habagat could start carving his anting-antings out, but Kidlat only gave her his usual cold stare.

"Oh! You better start with the healing first and the pain relief."

"Oh, Goddess of War, I didn't know you were so wicked!" Datu Habagat sneered.

At another time, Bulan would have punished Datu Habagat for such disrespectful words. Fear flashed in Kidlat's eyes for a moment. Bulan pushed Kidlat down onto the ground, faceup, and stepped on his wrist. He lay still.

"Have you talked to Putot?" Bulan asked Una. Una's wounds faded fast, so her healing must have been enhanced by Linog's power.

"No. I can't talk to anyone. Something must have happened to her." Worry crossed Una's face for a moment, but she smiled as she looked down upon Kidlat. She shook her head at Datu Habagat. "No, you don't. He's mine."

"He tried to kill my son." Datu Habagat stepped on Kidlat's other arm.

Bulan walked away, disgusted by the pleased expression on Datu Habagat and Una's faces.

"He killed Dasig." Una stepped on Kidlat's wrist Bulan had just left free.

"Datu Habagat," Bulan said in a serious tone. "Bugna got her tracker from your shaman, not Putot. Can you talk to her?"

"No." Datu Habagat mouthed some names. "Nobody's answering. Something is happening." The creases in his forehead deepened. "It looks like the trackers aren't working."

"Let's disarm Kidlat fast," Bulan said. "He needs to be stripped of all his anting-antings." She started by pulling away his head scarf, decorated with powerful anting-antings. She also untied his loincloth. Bulan couldn't help averting her eyes when the man had been stripped down naked. "I'll merge with my spirit and journey to the underworld to wake Bakunawa up."

"Who says you could barge into my territory, dear Bulan?" The words came out of Kidlat's mouth, but she knew the deep voice belonged to Dilim, the god of the underworld.

"Oh, but you already stepped into the land of the living, which you are clearly prohibited from visiting." Bulan's heart drummed, and she hoped her voice sounded strong.

"I came only to collect what's mine... which the

treaty says I can do freely. You have conveniently used my concealers for your advantage."

The snare ball in her hand stirred. Bulan gripped it tightly.

"That"—Kidlat stared at the snare ball—"is mine."

"Not the soul inside."

"Fair enough. But it'll be mine in two weeks."

Two weeks. Two weeks had passed since Bakunawa died. The soul would be Dilim's property a moon after a person's death, and Bakunawa was half human. Of course he wasn't there to collect the souls who had wreaked havoc. He was only interested in the concealers and Bakunawa. "You'll have it in two weeks."

"But you, my dear, aren't welcome in my domain. You should know that." Dilim laughed. "It'd be a violation of the treaty."

Bulan swallowed hard. She looked at Datu Habagat and Una. "Start now." Her thread of life was burning. She'd been holding onto her spirit for a long time and needed to let go. She took a deep breath and walked through the veil protecting the lake of life. The moment she entered, the stone in her hand turned gray. *Of course. This is the lake of life, where Dilim's power is weak.* She turned around, grabbed Kidlat's leg, and pulled him in. Before he could stand, she extended both hands to pull Una and Datu Habagat in also.

"What is this place?" Una asked.

"A place where Dilim can't do his tricks." Bulan's thread of life was at the point of snapping. Before she let go, two souls left the stone in her hand. One hovered over Bakunawa, as if trying to reunite. She rushed to Bakunawa's side after ejecting her spirit. "This is your body. Return."

Bakunawa's body remained unmoving.

Datu Habagat stood, eyes fixed on his son. "He needs a returning ceremony. I can do it." He walked away from Kidlat as if the man he hated wasn't there. "Charcoal. Fire." His eyes bulged as he looked around. He dove and grabbed some charcoal from where Bugna had done a ceremony almost two weeks before.

"Datu Habagat," Bulan said, feeling calm after dipping her toes in the magical water. "There are two souls. I think the body isn't ready to receive the spirit. You must return the mortal soul first."

Datu Habagat nodded furiously. Carefully, the datu pulled Bakunawa's upper body to dry ground but kept his feet touching the water that kept him alive. There, Datu Habagat performed a returning ceremony. Bulan stared unblinking, hoping Bakunawa would open his eyes. She tried to block out Kidlat's groaning and averted her eyes, not wanting to see Una's cruelty. When Bakunawa finally opened his eyes, she hurried to his side and helped him sit. Their eyes met.

Bulan hugged him. "Thank you for coming back, Bakunawa."

20

THE BOLO WARRIOR

"It wasn't just a dream," Makanas said.

Lin-ay kept calling him Bakunawa. He'd dreamt about Bakunawa and the afterlife. It felt incredibly real. He looked around in confusion and awe as he saw the tree in the middle of the lake. He stood on unsteady legs and bowed to Datu Habagat. "Thank you for helping me get back." Memories of the datu's cruelty returned. "But that doesn't erase your sins."

Datu Habagat simply nodded. Makanas was glad the datu didn't try to touch him. He wouldn't know how to react if the datu showed any emotion. He turned and saw Una... She... She was slicing Kidlat's arm open.

"What are you doing?" He started to run over to stop her, but Lin-ay grabbed his hand.

"I don't know where to start," Lin-ay said. "You don't know about the horrible things Kidlat had done. And you have a lot of things to know about yourself."

"That doesn't justify the cruelty. She'll be no better than him."

"We don't have a choice anyway!" Una said. "The anting-antings are absorbed in his body. We have to carve them out."

Makanas remembered Kidlat's words. The head warrior had ordered Makanas to carve the concealer out of his body if he died. Back then, he didn't think he would have to do it.

"Give him his pain reliever anting-anting, at least," Makanas said.

"Where's the fun in that?" Una answered.

"Una!" Makanas bellowed.

"He killed Dasig! He made Dasig suffer."

Speechless, Makanas couldn't do anything other than hold Lin-ay's hand, wondering how Kidlat could've killed Dasig, Makanas's closest friend and fellow warrior.

"And he killed many more," Una continued. "He opened the gate to the underworld. Thousands are dying because of him. Just so that people would follow him. They had to swear allegiance or die."

Makanas grabbed the hilt of Datu Habagat's sword. "Then let me cut off his head." He swung the blade up but then realized that must have been what Bugna saw. She had warned him not to kill his father.

"I'm sure you want to hear Dilim's message first…" Kidlat paused, obviously enjoying the shock on their faces. He was buying time, perhaps, playing with their emotions. And if Kidlat was truly powerful enough for the evil god of the underworld to choose him as an ally, then killing him was the obvious choice.

"Stop," Bulan said.

Makanas had no choice but to bring his blade down to his side. Kidlat sat up straight. Una let him move, but her eyes didn't leave his hands, tied behind him.

"He said the only way for Bakunawa to live as a demigod again is to merge in the afterlife." Kidlat chuckled. "In his domain."

Makanas didn't understand why they would want Bakunawa alive. He must have been unconscious for a long time for such a thing to develop.

"Play the messenger all you want. I don't care. You're going to meet your good friend soon." Bulan nudged Makanas, who moved to kill Kidlat.

"Ah! One more thing!" Kidlat said.

Makanas let him make his revelation.

"Dilim came to collect what's his. That includes the shaman Putot, Bugna, and all others who had consumed any power of the underworld. He stared at Datu Habagat. "Well, you're here because of that." His eyes moved down to the bakunawa blade strapped to Datu Habagat's waist. He said the power is too strong for him to pull. You'll follow them soon."

"Lies," Bulan said. "He can't claim the living."

"Yes, he can. He pulled them into the cave between worlds. They'd have been dead soon anyway."

Makanas's heart skipped a beat. Between worlds, beyond the gate to the underworld near Bugna's house, resided the evil people who had turned into monsters.

They had fought many of them before Bakunawa's rising.

"Wrong," Lin-ay gripped his hand tightly, her nails digging into his skin. "All he did was pull them between worlds. He has no power among the living. The boundary is Bakunawa's realm."

"Bakunawa couldn't even remember who he was." Kidlat laughed. "He'll be gone soon, and all those who sided with you, dear goddess of war. Did you tell your followers that you're nothing but a lower pantheon god?"

Una plunged a knife into Kidlat's stomach, and he didn't even struggle. She shared a look with Makanas. He was grateful he didn't have to kill him and be branded as a traitorous son who killed his father.

"Drag him out of the lake of life," Lin-ay ordered. "This place shouldn't be tainted with his dirty blood."

Lin-ay asked them all to hold hands. As they walked away from the lake, they passed through an invisible wall of power. His hair stood on end, and his whole body shook. When the feeling subsided, they let go of each others' hands.

There, Una slit Kidlat's throat, and he died with his eyes wide open.

"This bastard didn't have many anting-antings to carve out." Una wiped her knife against the grass. "His body absorbed most of them. But I made sure the healing is gone, so he can't come back from the afterlife."

"You... can detect anting-antings now?" Makanas asked, eyebrows raised.

"And more." Una raised a hand, and the ground before her swelled. "Wait... Lin-ay, why didn't you merge with your spirit?"

"I can't," Lin-ay said. "I have to journey to the underworld without my spirit. From now on, call me Bulan."

Makanas searched her eyes for signs of violence, but all he saw was Lin-ay, the girl he'd fallen in love with. He wondered if she managed to defeat Bulan and absorb her power.

"And Bakunawa," Lin-ay continued, "has a lot of things to learn. The journey will be long because we don't have Bugna. I need you to stay behind, stabilize the world of the living, and stop any more demons from coming out of the underworld. I'm sure Dilim only pulled those who could help us."

"But you need me," Una said. "If you are to face Dilim, you should be Bulan. Well, you decided you're already Bulan. What I mean is you should have your power as a demigod. With Linog's and Bagyo's power, I think we have a chance."

"No. We're only going between worlds, not to the underworld. If Dilim senses me there, he'll try to stop me. But if I go there as a human, he won't know it's me." Bulan rose into the air, carrying Makanas.

Makanas reminded himself to call her by her new name as she requested. Thinking of himself as Bakunawa as she had suggested, wasn't as easy.

"You could die!" Una rose as well, holding Datu Habagat's hand.

They flew quickly—faster than anyone Makanas had seen, aside from Bugna.

"Listen," Bulan said in a grave tone. "All I need is to get Bakunawa to where Bathala placed him. If I go there with my spirit, Dilim will ascend to the gods' realm and report my breach to Bathala."

"That's better!" Una said. "Bathala should fix the situation."

"Bathala isn't the kind of god humans think he is."

Makanas wondered what kind of god Bathala was. When people faced hardships, they normally said, "Leave it to Bathala," hoping the supreme god would make everything better. After all, he was the most powerful god and the creator.

"Bathala"—Bulan inhaled sharply—"could obliterate the whole of humanity if he thought it was too much to handle."

"That's just ridiculous." Una huffed. "So now what, you have all the power, but you're throwing it away and playing dead or alive with Dilim?"

"If I merge with my spirit now, I don't know how to expel it. It took Bathala and the gods a great deal of effort to separate it from my soul thousands of years ago."

As Una and Bulan argued, Makanas simply listened. He missed Dasig and the company of other warriors, but he couldn't be any happier about being with Bulan. She explained what had happened to him, how he lost his consciousness, and how he remained dead for two weeks. Makanas couldn't believe that he was Bakunawa, but the dream he'd had just before waking up was terrifying. He hoped that when the time came to merge with Bakunawa, he would be as strong as Bulan. As the warm setting sun caressed their backs, silence fell among them. They had survived Bakunawa's rising, but the fight was far from over.

Thank you for reading. If you liked The Bolo Warrior, please leave a review on Amazon. Your review will help other readers discover my book.

Also by AA Lee!

- The Priestess Trials Book 1
- High Priestess: The Priestess Trials Book 2
- Torch of Greed: The Priestess Trials Book 3
- The Priestess Trials Boxed Set

Made in United States
North Haven, CT
14 April 2022